The Sylvia Trap

Elizabeth Heij

The Sylvia Trap
and other short shorts

The Sylvia Trap and other short shorts
ISBN 978 1 76109 227 5
Copyright © Elizabeth Heij 2021
Cover image: pastel sketch by Elizabeth Heij

First published 2021 by
GINNINDERRA PRESS
PO Box 3461 Port Adelaide 5015
www.ginninderrapress.com.au

Contents

Foreword

I enjoy reading novels, but have not yet found the stickability to write one. My mind is like a butterfly that alights here and there on a whole range of topics, real or imagined, from remote past to unknown future.

This collection of short and micro stories arises from imagination working on snippets of ideas gleaned across the times and places of my life. Many have an underlying autobiographical origin, but even they are fictionalised. They are not intended as a factual record, but as places where your thoughts, like mine, can come to play and dance.

If you find at the end of a busy day that just a few minutes of reading are sufficient to leave the day's thoughts behind and induce sleep, then these stories are for you.

I am grateful to my family who, over the years, have provided love, humour, and all sorts of happenings and emotions that inform my writing.

And I am grateful to members of the University of the Third Age Aldinga, Creative Writing Group, for inspirational topic suggestions and honest, helpful critique of results.

My writing is generously supported by my husband, John, with many cups of coffee and an appreciation of the nature of 'creative space'.

Elizabeth Heij

The Sylvia trap

I used to be such a cocky young upstart. When I think back, I cringe at how naive I was. I had all the answers: find a job – tick; buy a car – tick; move into my own flat – tick! I even looked down on my school friends who were still living at home and either trying to make grades at uni, or out hunting for good jobs. While my job as a mechanic's apprentice was not what you would call high-class, I was convinced I was doing better than my mates. What an idiot I was!

Well, cocky young bucks come unstuck eventually, and I did too. It happened because I didn't have any idea of how to deal with someone like Sylvia. She turned up with another girl at my twenty first, and she was an eye-popper. I was reduced to stammering shyness.

There I was, glass of beer in my hand, when in came this gorgeous vision, with long, honey-coloured hair, big blue eyes, a golden tan, and long slim legs under a red miniskirt.

One of the other girls tapped her glass for quiet and announced, 'Hi, everyone. This is Sylvia. Her family just moved in nearby. She'd love to meet new friends.'

I was hooked. I had instant visions of driving around with this glorious girl beside me in my car, taking her on dates, and getting to know her better – very much better – at my flat! I edged my way across to where she was standing.

Bertie, who was already talking to her, introduced us. 'This is Richie, the birthday boy. He's got his own car, so he's a really useful friend.'

Sylvia must have made a note of that as, later in the evening, she came over and asked if I could take her home in my car. Could I ever!

When we reached her house, she asked me to go to the beach with her the next day. Oh boy – we were getting on like a house on fire. Well,

I was on fire for sure! She made a time for me to pick her up the next day, and then said goodnight with an intimate squeeze of my arm.

Getting to spend the next day at the beach was a problem. It was a work day, and the boss was a mean, annoying so-and-so. He was a scrooge about pay, fussy about time worked and always looking over everyone's shoulder. I knew he wouldn't give me a day off unless I was half dead so, obviously, that's what I would have to be!

First thing in the morning, I called work and pleaded a severe case of gastro with vomiting all over the place. Naturally, they didn't want me around in that state, so it seemed I was free to pick up Sylvia and spend a marvellous day lying in the sun ogling and flirting.

I was disappointed when she chose Wattle Bay as our destination. It's always so crowded. I had in mind somewhere much more secluded! Well, never mind. It was still a date with a gorgeous girl.

We reached the beach and changed into our swimsuits. Oh sweet Jesus! When Sylvia emerged from the change rooms she had on a tiny – and I mean tiny – red bikini looking stunning against her golden tan.

I think my jaw must have nearly hit my knees because she looked at me and laughed, 'What's the matter, Richie? Surely you've seen a bikini before!'

In a haze of lust, I wrapped my towel around my waist and followed her down to find a place to lie in the sun.

Well, that initial vision of Sylvia in her bikini was the high point of the day. It only went downhill from there. There was no privacy for getting to know each other. It seemed she was making new friends all over the beach – male friends – for whom I was invisible. While I went off several times during the day to buy her drinks and snacks, it made no difference. Sylvia was continuously occupied by other guys wanting to sit and talk.

The last straw was when one good-looking surfie type came and asked if she would like a ride home in his new MG sports car – a two-seater of course. She squealed happily and agreed; then turned to me, thanked me prettily for a nice day, picked up her things and ran off after him.

Glumly, I picked up my own stuff and went back to my car. But fate had a final blow to deliver.

Just as I was opening the car door, my annoying boss drove past. He slowed down and called from his window, 'Well, Richie, I see you've got over the gastro. See you in my office first thing tomorrow.'

Magic in a mundane task

The air is hot and humid under a misty-blue sky. The monsoon is still some time off but already the weight of moisture in the air enforces a slower pace. The river beyond the walls of the old Mughal palace is sluggish, its flow seemingly almost oily as it moves across the land. Leaves hang motionless in the afternoon heat. Birds and insects are silent waiting for the cooler dusk.

An old man sits cross-legged under a neem tree smoking a hookah. His casual turban and dhoti are the colour of old ivory, ingrained with the dust of the plains. Except for a trickle of smoke and the occasional rise and fall of his hand, he sits quietly in the shade, watching his grandson mowing the courtyard lawn.

The boy, who must be around five years old, walks slowly across the grass behind a placid grey Brahmin cow, occasionally tapping her lightly on the rump with a long, thin whisk as if to let her know he is following. He is barefoot, in frayed kurta pyjamas that were once white but are now a mix of grubby grey, with patches of green and brown suggesting many encounters with the lawn and cow. His hair, glinting almost blue-black in the sun, flops over his forehead in a bowl cut.

The cow, as she moves serenely across the lawn, tows a gently whirring reel mower which throws cut grass into a catcher behind. Perhaps, years ago, you might have mowed the lawn with a similar hand mower and catcher. This mower is a little wider but, with the cow providing the motive power, a lot less work.

At the end of the traverse, the cow stops. The boy unhitches the grass catcher, walks around the cow and empties the grass into a pile in front of her. She begins to eat this welcome snack, encouraged by a pat on the neck from her little master. The boy walks over to his grandfather and sits down beside him, whisking his stick back and forth in the manner of small boys everywhere.

As the cow finishes eating the pile of clippings, she lifts her tail and, with a wet flop, deposits a cowpat. The boy gets up and walks back towards her. He takes a flat wooden scoop from a large basket by the wall of the courtyard, picks up the deposit, and adds it to the contents of the basket. Returning to the cow, he reattaches the grass catcher and, by gently pulling on her harness, turns her round to face the other way across the lawn. The cow knows this routine well. Without any encouragement from the whisk, she peacefully puts one foot in front of the other and heads in a straight line for the other side. Occasional light taps of the whisk remind her of her task and direction.

At the other side, the boy turns her again and she sets off once more. Again, the pile of clippings is dropped for her, and the boy walks off towards his grandfather under the tree. This time, he picks up a bowl from the ground beside his grandfather. He walks back to the cow and places the bowl beneath her. Squatting beside her, he gently pats her udder then, milking her expertly, sends a frothing stream into the bowl. The cow munches on. Standing up, the boy takes a long drink from the bowl, then carefully carries the remainder over to his grandfather, who momentarily lays down his hookah, drains the bowl and upends it on the grass beside him. The boy returns to guide the cow into another traverse of the lawn.

I have been so taken with the scene before me that the tour group is now out of sight along the path towards the main palace building. Reluctantly, I turn and follow. The building is, of course, magnificent, as are all the old structures of the former Mughal empire, but I can't remember much of it. For the remainder of the afternoon, my mind is taken up with the perfect, beautiful synergy of the lawnmowing scene.

The boy knows the cow is a sacred fellow being, and should only give her labour and milk voluntarily, in return for care and kindness. Although the grass has been eaten by the cow, the lawn looks carefully manicured as visitors expect, rather than randomly grazed. The collected cowpats, probably destined to be garden fertiliser or fuel, will not create a hazard for picnickers on the lawn. The boy and his grandfather have received a healthy drink of milk, and spent time with each other in unhurried togetherness. I compare this perfect synergy, this Zen of lawn mowing, with the noisy, smelly, motorised process of mowing lawns in Australian suburbia.

No contest!

A wanderer drops in

Years ago, when there were such jobs to be had, I was working for a coastal shipping company as captain of the *Fortitude*, a small diesel freighter running mixed cargo between Hobart and the other east coast ports. *Fortitude* was a good name for her. She was old, dirty and rust-streaked, but otherwise seaworthy – a tough, hard-working, little tub of a ship.

I remember taking her through some hard winter storms off Bass Strait, a stretch of water which competes with New Zealand's Cook Strait for the title 'Windpipe of the World'. One such storm blew up out of the south-west as we were steaming down the east coast of Tasmania on approach to Hobart. We were scheduled to make port before nightfall, but it quickly became clear this was not going to be possible. If such weather had happened further north, it would have been called a cyclone.

The wind screamed like a banshee around the superstructure of the ship, and the sea surface quickly became a maelstrom of stinging spray and white foaming rollers taller than the ship's radio mast. There was nothing we could do but try to ride it out. We turned the ship's bow into the wind, keeping just enough power on her to hold her heading in the hope we could avoid being blown out east into the Tasman.

So there we sat, battering our way into huge breaking waves that swept over the bow, frothed along the deck and swept over the stern. The bow pointed skyward as each wave took us, cresting to the sound of racing engines as the screw came out of the water, then swooped down into the following trough with a shuddering crash.

As the day gave way to twilight, there was still no let-up in the gale. It looked as though we were in for an evil night.

Just as twilight had almost given way to darkness, there was a thud on the left wing of the bridge and a flash of white showed briefly through the side window. I asked Andy, my young offsider on watch, to take the wheel while I went to check it out.

Well, what a surprise! There, huddled down behind the screen on the leading side was a gigantic, bedraggled white bird with black-flecked wings and a large pink beak – a wandering albatross. I knew the bird well from seeing it in the air and occasionally spotting it feeding on the water. Strangely, what first came to mind was Samuel Taylor Coleridge's poem 'The Rime of the Ancient Mariner'. The albatross was a bird that one wouldn't want to mistreat! This one was soaked and exhausted after battling a gale for who knew how long. Normally, these birds rest on the water, but the heaving, foaming water now around us was no place for a bird to take a break!

As I looked at him, he turned his head and looked at me with one beady eye, as if pleading to be left alone to weather the storm in the meagre shelter of the bridge screen. Although he was wet, bedraggled and undoubtedly tired, he appeared to be otherwise uninjured. When I returned to the main bridge and told Andy, he couldn't resist taking a look also.

We decided to leave the albatross where he was until the gale moderated. We did wonder how such a big bird with such a huge wingspan was going to take to the air again from behind the screens of the bridge, but we had a storm to weather first.

In the morning, when Andy and I came back on watch, the storm was beginning to abate. We carefully put the *Fortitude* back on course for Hobart and peered out onto the bridge wing to check on the albatross. He was still there, now standing on large pink feet, pacing around and shuffling his wings as though he wanted to get back into the air. It was obviously a problem, as the space behind the screen was too small to extend his enormously long wings.

Andy and I agreed that desperate times called for desperate measures. We would approach him, one each side, grab his wings and bundle him over the edge of the bridge into the open air.

Well, he was one heavy load of bird, but we did it. That beautiful wild creature cooperated magnificently. He made no objection to being picked up and thrown off the ship. He simply looked at us, allowed us to lift him, then opened his amazing wings and soared into the air. After a farewell circuit close above us, he departed away to the east.

The experience made a big impression on us. It was rare to experience what seemed like true understanding with a creature from the wild. I kept thinking about his eye that looked at me, first when he dropped in out of the storm, and then when he accepted our help to get airborne again.

That silent communication, perhaps directly with my soul, was the reason I recorded a verse along with the incident in the ship's log. I still have the page:

I am a spirit of life primeval, born from an endless today.
I am the voice of the storm and the waters, a child of the white sea spray.
Fill my wings with the winds of the heavens, and my heart with the light of the sky.
Spread the sea like a carpet below me, and lift me aloft to fly.

A blast of a party!

Teenage cousins Nick and Chris are discussing their invitations to Auntie May's birthday party.

'Are you going?' Nick asks Chris.

'Mum says I should,' Chris answers. 'It might be the last birthday Auntie ever has.'

'How old is she, anyway?' asks Nick. 'She looks ancient, and Dad says she's our grandma's big sister, so she must be old.'

'She's ninety-four,' says Chris. 'I know because Mum bought two birthday candles shaped like numbers, a 9 and a 4, and I know for sure she isn't forty-nine!'

Nick thinks for a moment. 'Man, it's going to be so boring – a party full of old fogies and only two candles on the cake. Can't we liven it up somehow?'

Now it's Chris's turn to think. 'It would be nice if there could be ninety-four candles on the cake for real but it would be too slow and difficult for anyone to light them all before the first ones burn down to the cake, and Auntie's really shaky these days, so she would never be able to blow them all out in one go.'

There is silence for a while as the two consider the problem and take turns swigging a can of Coke.

'I know,' says Nick excitedly. 'We can use that old barrel lid to make a big stand to go under the cake, and put all the candles around it in a circle. Your mum can still use her number candles on the cake itself.'

Now Chris's creative spirit is really fired up. 'Yes. And if we can use little flames, not real candles, they can be lit quickly and all put out in one go too. What about if we make a hollow space under the barrel lid and put little tubes through to act as candles, then hitch the whole thing up to the barbecue gas bottle?'

'Wow,' says Nick. 'That would be really cool. We could turn on the gas, then light the little jets with a wave of one big candle. And we could give Auntie a pretend magic wand to wave to turn them off. We can stand behind the table and turn off the gas at the bottle when she waves it. There would be only two real candles to blow out, and I reckon Auntie could do that. Whatcha think?'

'Oh man!' says Chris, chuckling. 'That's a gas for sure. Let's do it. There's plenty of stuff in our garage. Dad's a real hoarder.'

For the next couple of weekends, the two friends are shut in the garage working up their idea. In spite of family curiosity about noises of sawing, hammering and clanging metal, no one is allowed in. The boys carefully defend their surprise for Auntie.

On the day of the party, the boys are out early helping Chris's mum get the big garden room ready and position the cake. She knows the boys have built a nice round white-painted stand to put the cake on. The ninety-four little decorative silver tubes around its rim look very pretty – a bit like real candles. She has no idea they're more than they seem, and hasn't looked beneath the long white table cloth to spot the gas bottle under the table.

Now the party is in full swing. The room is a crush of guests eating, drinking, laughing and congratulating Auntie, who sits grinning in a wheelchair beside the big table with its crowning glory of a cake.

As the toasts and congratulations finish, Chris and Nick take up their positions behind the cake and surreptitiously attach the tube from the gas bottle to the connector in the stand beneath the cake.

Chris's mum lights the two candles on the top of the cake and, just as everyone is about to sing 'Happy Birthday', Chris says, 'Hang on a minute. I have a special candle and a real magic wand for Auntie.'

He whips a long white candle out from under the tablecloth, and a silver-painted stick with a silver star on the end. He gives Auntie the wand, then lights the candle with a lighter, and holds it up high.

While everyone is looking at the candle, Nick turns on the gas bottle under the table. Chris waits a few seconds to let the gas fill the chamber in the cake stand, and then waves the candle flame over the little tubes around the platter.

Boooom!

Nick and Chris are knocked over, the fancy curtains over the table go up in flames, Auntie's chair rolls backward with Auntie grinning, cackling and waving her wand.

'Quick!' yells someone. 'Call the fire brigade!'

From Soci-Histori (AD 2556) – the history of CASS

Definition: CASS – Contagious Abortion and Sterilisation Syndrome.

Some five hundred years ago, in the year 2024, a pig farmer in what was then eastern Australia noticed that a number of his breeding sows seemed unwell, and several had aborted their litters. As sows then averaged ten to twelve piglets per litter, total loss could have serious financial implications.

A local animal health expert, at the time called a vet, could find no reason for the abortions but, to be on the safe side, he quarantined the farm and imposed strict hygiene measures. Dead piglets, waste from the sow stalls, and uneaten food were all put into deep pits on the farm, covered with waste oil, burned and buried. Staff were sent home as a precaution. No one knew if the infection might be contagious to humans.

As days passed, more pigs became unwell and more litters were aborted. Finally, the vet contacted the National Animal Health Authority for help. Their experts also were unable to identify the infectious agent beyond saying it appeared to be a virus, probably newly emerging. As a precaution, they ruled that all pigs on the farm should be slaughtered, burned and buried on site, with compensation being made available to the farmer. Once that was done, authorities hoped the problem would be over. To avoid panic in the pork market, there was no release of news to the press at the time.

Unfortunately, following this incident, one of the farm workers and his wife developed flu-like symptoms. The husband passed it on to several friends, and the wife passed it on to her sister, who was pregnant. Tragically, the sister not only developed the same flu-like symptoms but also suffered a miscarriage; as did the wife of one of the husband's friends.

It soon became clear that the previously unknown virus was spreading fast nationwide. It was highly contagious in humans as well as pigs, with the frightening symptom of causing infected pregnant females to abort.

Authorities tried to keep a lid on the news to avoid mass panic, but the news couldn't be contained. There was indeed mass panic. Pregnant women tried to quarantine their households and refuse all contacts – to no avail. The horrifying new virus spread as easily as colds and flu – through the air, on contaminated surfaces and via doctors' consulting rooms.

Affected individuals almost all recovered but pregnancy losses were widespread. It appeared there was little natural immunity in the population; and generating a vaccine might take many years of research – even supposing it might be possible.

The virus quickly spread to other countries via air travel. Birth rates everywhere dropped precipitously and world population forecasts were revised downwards. Then, to make matters worse, another horrifying symptom emerged. Human miscarriages, although tragic, were not the most sinister symptom. Gradually it became clear that women who contracted the virus in their child-bearing years could never afterwards conceive a child. In desperation, women tried to adopt. However, women who managed to carry babies to term were all either keeping their infants or demanding huge sums for making them available for adoption. World population forecasts were revised downwards yet again. Doomsayers began predicting the end of the human race.

But, of course, Nature's host-parasite laws always allow for survival. Slowly it emerged that, in every country, a small proportion of individuals were resistant to the virus. Babies continued to be born, albeit in very low numbers to begin with, until resistance increased generation by generation. Economists warned that the tiny number of surviving young people could not possibly support the enormous older generation as they aged – a truth that was patently obvious. The emergence of resistance, however, buoyed everyone's hopes for the future, and they pulled together in a manner not seen previously. The older generation adopted creative cooperation as a way of life and devised many new ways to support themselves through their advancing years.

The final outcome was a population less than one quarter the size it had been before the CASS pandemic, with many more resources and opportunities available to those born afterwards. Forests, fish and other threatened wildlife returned. Global warming halted and began to reverse. Instead of using over fifty per cent of the Earth's photosynthetic product, humanity returned to using less than twenty per cent.

In historical hindsight, CASS was a personal tragedy for many would-be parents, but a miraculous rescue for a species that was patently breeding itself to death. There was, of course, worldwide political and economic chaos for over four decades as old systems broke down and new ways of living were invented. Gradually, however, order returned to social systems. This time, unlike the period after the bubonic plague in the fourteenth century, humanity learned a lesson in sustainable breeding behaviour that it never forgot.

Baxter finds a friend

Andy and his mum are moving into a new neighbourhood. On moving day, they introduce themselves to an elderly lady who has come out onto the porch next door to see who her new neighbours are. Andy sees she has a big dog beside her. He has a shiny black coat, big paws, a wide grin and a tail that seems to be wagging from the neck down.

'Hello,' says Andy's mum. 'I'm Julie Jarret and this is my boy Andy. He'll be ten next birthday.'

'Hello,' says the elderly lady, leaning on the porch railing. 'I'm Mrs Mercer. I live here on my own since my husband died two years ago. And this is Baxter. He's a Labrador, so he's very friendly. You won't need to worry about him. He's only just a year old so really not much more than a pup. My son gave him to me when my poor old spaniel died. He sometimes barks if someone comes up the front path, but it's not a fierce back, just a bit of a woof to tell me there's someone about.'

Andy kneels down to make friends with Baxter, who is only too happy to oblige.

Mrs Mercer smiles at the sight of Andy getting a good licking. 'He likes you, young man. No trouble there!'

As the weeks pass, Andy is feeling more at home in his new school and the new neighbourhood. He soon finds he can say hello to Baxter over the backyard fence, and Baxter always seems keen to give a friendly woof and tail wag.

One day, he says to his mum, 'Do you think Mrs Mercer would let me go over and play with Baxter? I'm sure I could teach him to play fetch.'

'Why don't you ask her, dear,' says his mum.

So Andy goes over to Mrs Mercer's front door, knocks and asks her.

'Of course you can play with Baxter,' she says, 'and I'll show you a secret way to get from your backyard into mine so you can play with him whenever he's in the yard. It can be like going through the wardrobe to Narnia. He really needs more exercise, and playing fetch would be good for him. I'm getting too old to take him for walks and, to tell you the truth, I worry he might knock me over when he gets all playful and jumps up like a mad kangaroo.'

Mrs Mercer takes Andy through her house into the backyard. Baxter is very excited and runs around them in circles leaping and bouncing like a black jack-in-the-box.

Mrs Mercer takes Andy down to the back of the garden near the end of the fence between their two backyards. A jungle of creepers is hanging over the fence.

'Look behind all that green stuff,' she says. 'There should be an old gate under there. If you cut the creepers back a bit, you should be able to use it OK.'

Andy burrows into the heavy mass of creepers and is delighted to find a little gate.

'Here it is, and the latch is still working. I can tie the creepers back enough to get through.' He checks it out by squeezing through to his own backyard and then back to Mrs Mercer's place.

Baxter is delighted by this new development and starts snuffling and digging at the base of the gate.

'Look, Mrs Mercer,' says Andy. 'Baxter's helping me clear the gateway. Can I play with him now and then go home through the gate when we've finished?'

'Of course you can, dear,' says Mrs Mercer. She walks slowly back to the house, using the porch handrail to help climb the steps to the back door.

Andy stays until his mum calls him for tea. It's the start of a great friendship. Every day after school, if it's not actually raining, Andy is next door playing with Baxter.

After a few weeks, Andy tells his mum, 'Baxter's doing really well. He's really bright. He fetches his stick right to my feet every time, and he can sit, lie down, roll over and shake hands when I tell him. He woofs when I tell him to speak too.'

Mum says, 'That's very clever of you both, and Mrs Mercer is very happy. She's seen out of the window all the things you've taught him to do. And she's especially happy now that he sits quietly in front of the fire with her at night after having plenty of exercise.'

The boy–dog friendship progresses happily, with Andy sometimes taking Baxter out for a walk on the lead to do some simple shopping for Mrs Mercer. Baxter has now learned to walk quietly on the lead beside Andy rather than bounding around him like a jumping jack. Andy enjoys the occasional ice cream treat Mrs Mercer lets him buy on a really hot day, and Baxter enjoys the little bit at the bottom of the cone that Andy shares with him.

One day, when Andy comes into the yard, Baxter is behaving strangely. He stands by the back door whining and won't come down into the yard to play.

'What's the matter, boy?' says Andy. 'Do you want to go inside?' He opens the door and the dog shoots through it, his claws scrabbling on the kitchen linoleum. Andy follows Baxter's whining and barking. He is horrified to find Baxter nuzzling the face of Mrs Mercer, who is lying still and grey in the hallway near the front door.

'Mum, Mum,' Any calls as he runs out the door and across to his own house. 'Come quickly. Mrs Mercer needs help. She's lying on the floor not moving.'

Andy's Mum grabs her phone and runs next door with Andy. She checks that Mrs Mercer is breathing and calls for an ambulance to come quickly. She gets Andy to help her turn Mrs Mercer on her side and put a blanket over her.

'Don't worry, Baxter,' Andy says, patting the dog when it growls at the ambulance crew. 'They'll take good care of her, and I'll take good care of you.'

He packs Baxter's bed and bowls into a big box and takes them home with him.

Baxter follows quietly. He seems to understand that it's not a time for games.

The next day, Andy's mum has a phone call from Mrs Mercer's son with a message from the hospital. 'Mrs Mercer has had a stroke,' she explains to Andy. 'That's some bleeding in the brain, but thanks to you calling so quickly for help, she's out of danger now.'

'Will she come home soon?' Any asks.

'I'm sorry, love,' says Andy's mum. 'She won't be able to look after herself at home any more so she has to go to a retirement home when she comes out of hospital. She wants to know if you would be willing to adopt Baxter because the home doesn't allow people to bring their pets. Would you like to do that?'

Now it's Andy's turn to be bounding around like a mad kangaroo. 'Can I really have Baxter to live with us? Can I really?'

'Yes, dear, you can. He can be your birthday present from Mrs Mercer; but you have to promise to take care of him – his feeding, exercise, baths and all that sort of stuff. And when Mrs Mercer is settled in her new home, she would love it if you could take Baxter to visit.'

'I promise. I promise. Oh, Mum, it's sad for Mrs Mercer but I feel like I just got the very best present ever.'

And there's Baxter, right beside him, grinning his doggie grin and wagging his tail from the neck down.

A few weeks later, when Baxter is used to living at Andy's place and Mrs Mercer is all set up in her new room at the retirement home, Andy's mum takes Andy and Baxter to visit her. Baxter and Mrs Mercer are very happy to see each other. When Mrs Mercer sees them at the door of the big lounge, her face lights up with a grin nearly as wide as Baxter's. Baxter bounds across the room and leaps around her doing his mad kangaroo act. She pats him fondly and introduces him and Andy to the other residents sitting in the lounge.

'Oooh, isn't he lovely,' they say. 'What a beautiful dog.' 'How shiny his coat is.' 'He really looks as though he's grinning at us.' 'Can we pat him?'

Andy takes Baxter around the room for shake hands and pats. What a treat this is for Mrs Mercer and the other residents. They think Baxter is wonderful, and Baxter is having a great time too. Soon everyone in the room has a wide grin to match Baxter's.

Andy's mum can see all the happy faces. Yes, she thinks. Andy and I should make this a regular treat.

So they do!

David thought he was dead

David thought he was dead – but that was only later when he could think at all.

At first, there was only a vague sense of 'I am', wrapped inside soft, impenetrable, black nothingness – no light, no sound, no smell, no sensation of touch, only a faint spark of self-awareness floating in infinite darkness.

He existed. It was enough. The spark of consciousness floated peacefully. Time passed.

Gradually, he became aware of a rhythm, a slow pulse, felt as well as heard. He dwelt on it, was moved by it and embraced it. He had a heartbeat. Time passed.

Some time later, he opened his eyes. He could feel his eyelids as he raised and lowered them but the total darkness remained. He tried to flex his fingers, but could feel no response, no sensation of touch. It was enough for now. Time passed.

Then awareness grew, and he became mindful of the blackness around him, but found no sign of anything that his senses could register. A wave of panic overwhelmed him. His heartbeat became a frantic drumroll in his ears and a pounding throb within his being. Sharp needles of sheer terror lanced through him. This wasn't any recognisable manifestation of life. He must be dead. Death was not heaven, not hell, but eternal black nothingness. He was overcome by a fear so great he couldn't bear it. His consciousness curled up in a ball and hid from the fear. He slept. Time passed.

Later, he floated back to awareness knowing he still lived – but how and where? He became conscious of faint pearly light, barely perceptible at first but gradually growing in intensity. Now he could see, but the perception made no sense. Surely there should be sky far above, not this vague arch of pearly whiteness close around him.

Then he could hear – a gentle rise and fall of human sounds. It became more audible and took on meaning, repeating over and over, 'David, it's time to wake up.'

For a moment, he was a child again with his mother calling him to breakfast. He listened, but could not decide how to respond. The voice continued. Time passed.

Later, the light became brighter and the voice more insistent. It was a man's voice repeating, 'David, we're going to open your capsule now.'

The pearly whiteness above him became a window with vague shapes behind it. He could see human forms dressed in white against a background of darker shapes.

Then, with frightening suddenness, the window over him slid away, leaving him unprotected in a newly perceived world. Hands reached down towards him and began working outside his field of view, but now within his sense of touch. He felt movement in forgotten arms and legs. Briefly, he flailed until he remembered how to control them. Hands steadied him as gravity returned and the sensation of floating departed. He was lying on a stretcher, which the hands now lifted from the capsule and transferred to a nearby bed.

Crackling thermal blankets were placed over him. Someone turned his head to the side, placed a straw in his mouth and told him to drink. It took a few moments to remember how to suckle but, as a basic human instinct, it soon came back. He drank a warm sweet liquid that seemed to fill him with the pleasure of living.

He struggled to sit up and someone adjusted the top half of the bed to help him. As he finished his drink, he watched the activity around his capsule. White-coated figures worked with the tubes, restraints, wires and controls, finally closing the translucent lid and turning off the power. His former little world was dark and silent again.

His bed was wheeled to a hospital-style room. Someone placed a number of sticky patches on his scalp and chest. More wires were connected. A couple of uncomfortable tubes were inserted. Then he was left to sleep. Time passed.

When he awoke, he could finally understand. He was David Oldenburg, NASA volunteer, the first trial subject in development of suspended animation for space travel. As he was still alive and now felt normal, it appeared the trial had been successful.

A man in a white coat entered the room holding a scroll of computer printout. This time, he recognised the man as Dr Ormond Dyson, the trial supervisor.

'How are you feeling, David? If you're OK, I hope you can answer a question to help us analyse your bio-data.' He laid the printout on the bed in front of David. 'See these sudden, abnormally high peaks in brain activity and heart rate – have you any recollection of what might have caused them?'

'Yes,' said David. 'That would have been when I thought I was dead. It was pure and absolute terror. You need to change the reanimation sequence so it can't happen again.'

Bernhardt remembers the Pied Piper

In the year of our Lord 1284, I was ten years old and living in the little town of Hamelin. My best friends – really my only friends – were Mathis and Frieda. Mathis was a year older than me and Frieda a year younger. We played together and kept to ourselves, away from the other children. They laughed at us because we couldn't join properly in their games.

Frieda was nearly blind. She could see light and tell where the sun was, but had to hold on to one of us when we walked around so she wouldn't bump into things. Mathis was so deaf he was always being startled by things that moved in the street. He couldn't hear us unless we yelled right into his ears or made signs he knew. I had to walk with the help of a big stick because my left foot was so twisted up behind my leg I couldn't put it on the ground to walk. So we were blind, deaf and lame, but we got on all right with each other and enjoyed our own different sorts of games and stories.

One day, a stranger came to town. We heard him before we saw him because he was playing wonderful tunes on a long wooden pipe. Well, Frieda and I heard him even though Mathis didn't. So I grabbed Frieda's hand and Mathis's hand and we followed the sound to the town square. There, we found the piper playing to a great crowd of townspeople, including all the children. He was sitting on the side of the fountain and playing like we never heard before. What a strange-looking man he was, all dressed in colourful, mismatched clothes with a tall stripy hat.

Every so often, he would stop playing and beckon the children to come closer to listen to stories. He was a great storyteller, fascinating us with tales of a wonderful country just beyond the mountain. Over there, he said, the sun always shone, there were endless delicious foods to eat, and no one had to wear ragged clothes or shoes that pinched. In the whole crowd of children, only Mathis was bored because he couldn't hear the music or stories properly, but we promised to tell him more about it all later. The grown-ups gradually left the square muttering about having too much to do to listen to fairy stories, and about how they could still listen to the music while they worked.

Once all the grown-ups had gone, the piper reached into the sack he carried on his back and took out a bag filled with delicious colourful sweets to pass around. There were enough for all the children, but Frieda, Mathis and I missed out because we were right at the back of the crowd and the other children never noticed us anyway.

Then the piper said to the crowd, 'How about we all dance. I know good music for dancing, so let's all dance in a long line, two-by-two. We'll go right around the town.'

He began piping, cheerful lively music that made your feet want to dance by themselves. The children jumped up and began to dance, wildly with lots of laughter. The piper stood up and led them out of the square into the streets of the town. We tried to follow but we could only go slowly. I was too lame to dance. Mathis couldn't hear the music to keep time to, and Frieda couldn't see where to put her feet down safely. We heard the piping and the laughter out in the streets for a while, then getting fainter and further away.

'Let's stay here in the square,' said Frieda. 'If they go around the town, surely they'll be back here later.'

So we waited in the square but, after a long time, we couldn't hear any piping or laughter at all. We waited until the sun was going down and some of the grown-ups came back to look for their children. They were grumbling about them staying too long and being late for supper. They asked us where they had gone but, of course, we couldn't tell them. We could only say we thought they were going to dance around the town and back.

Well, what a to-do there was! The townsfolk were running around like hens with a fox in the barnyard. They looked down every street and along the roads that went out through the town walls to the country-side. Lanterns were lit as it got dark, but there was still no sign of the children. Only the three of us, Mathis, Frieda and I, were left.

The grown-ups all went to the town church to light candles and pray that their children would return – but of course they never did.

A knock at the door

Late Victorian England

There was a knock on the door. I looked at George. Who could it be at this time of night?

George stood up and walked to the door. 'Who's there?' he asked.

The reply was soft, muffled by the door. There was a pause as George unbolted and opened it a crack. After some more soft conversation, he opened it fully.

'Come in, lad. You must be cold out there at this time of night. Come in and sit by the fire. We can give you some hot soup and you can tell us your tale.'

Into the room stepped a small, slender figure in a hooded coat. George followed, picking up a stool and setting it between our chairs in front of the fire.

'There you go. Sit down there and warm up. I'm George McMillan and this is my wife Elaine. Would you like a mug of soup?'

The stranger nodded. I went to the kitchen to fetch the last of our dinner-time soup. When I returned, the stranger had shed the coat and was looking around with interest.

I handed over the mug and a heel of bread, and returned to my chair.

'Thank you,' said the stranger. 'You're very kind.'

The accent was distinctly foreign. I looked again and gave a start, for this was no lad! While the short dark hair, trousers and slim figure suggested a boy, the voice was that of a girl, and the face that of a beautiful young woman with dark eyes and dusky skin.

George had come to the same conclusion. 'Oh my,' he said. 'I can see you're not a boy after all. Tell us about yourself, dear, and why you're walking around alone at night.'

The young woman took a sip of the soup, and then spoke. 'My name is Sunita. I know this will be a shock, but I think you could be my uncle. My father was Malcolm McMillan, a railway engineer from Glasgow. He told me long ago when my mother died that, if anything happened to him, I should go and find his brother George who worked the tin mines in Cornwall. Could that be you, Mr McMillan? The driver of the coach from Southampton told me there are a number of Scottish engineers working for the mines hereabouts. The lady in the Truro gift shop told me how to find you by name once I left the coach.'

George looked as stunned as I felt. 'Well,' he said, 'I did have a brother Malcolm who went to India with the army engineers long ago when we were little more than lads. There was an uprising near where he was working and then no further word. It seemed he might have been killed, but we could get no word from the army.'

Sunita reached into a pocket and pulled out an old photograph, folded and worn. She passed it to George. After looking at it, he appeared even more stunned if that were possible.

'Oh, my dear, this is such a shock. That's Malcolm and me with our parents when we were lads in Glasgow. It must have been taken just before he joined the army. You must indeed be my niece. We are so glad you found us. Please stay awhile so we can get to know each other.'

'That sounds wonderful,' replied Sunita, 'but before I answer, you need to know the rest of the story.' She pulled out another photograph and passed it to George. 'These are my parents. My mother's name was Sunaya.'

'Yes. That's definitely Malcolm,' he said, and passed it on to me.

The formal wedding photograph, also old and folded, showed a young couple in Indian wedding dress, the man in a turban and white coat with a sword at his side, the bride in a sari hung with coins and necklaces.

I could see Sunita's resemblance to her mother. Her mother's colouring was darker but otherwise they were very alike.

'You see,' said Sunita, 'I'm Anglo-Indian, and not everyone accepts half-castes. My parents were married only in the Punjabi tradition so, for many English people, I'm illegitimate.' She paused for a few moments and then continued.

'My father loved my mother so much he deserted the army to marry her and live secretly in the Punjabi mountains. Being a deserter meant he could never return to England. He passed for a well-born Indian native for the rest of his life. So I would love to accept your invitation to stay, if you can accept these other parts of my story.'

George and I rose from our chairs and hugged Sunita. 'Of course we accept you, dear. We're so glad you found us. Please stay as long as you wish – forever, if you like. There must be so much more to tell us.'

So that's how Sunita came into our lives like a gift of exotic sunshine.

Losing freedom and finding myself

When lockdowns and social distancing were introduced to slow the march of Covid-19, my first thoughts were about the frightening, alien and negative aspects of the situation. I was scared for myself, scared for family members, angry at dismissive politicians and frustrated with everyone who had stripped supermarket shelves of groceries I needed. Then, as bad news kept coming, I was furious at cruise ship operators who seemed determined to offload infected passengers at any cost. I was confronted by the apparent selfishness of individuals, particularly those in the younger generations, whose social lives were more important than public health, who assumed they were indestructible and who referred to the virus as the 'boomer remover'. I was fixated by the riveting, repetitive news on TV and the internet. My level of anxiety rose and sleep suffered. In short, I was a thoroughly frightened, grumpy old woman.

But then a strange thing began to happen. It started with just another piece of bad news, namely, that it would be at least a year to eighteen months before there was any hope of a vaccine, and probably even longer before mass vaccination trickled down to us. Maybe, as it is for the common cold virus, there never would be an effective vaccine. The concept of at least two years, or possibly the rest of my life, under extreme social distancing was confronting, a game changer. For someone of my age, this new lifestyle might be permanent, and I would have to learn to accept and live with it.

Along with gradual acceptance came an unexpected sense of freedom. I realised I was enjoying social distancing, relishing the peace and slower pace; grateful for relief from perceived pressure to socialise. It dawned on me that I've been in training for this new world all my life. I'm an extreme introvert by temperament, so the normal situation of operating in a world geared for extroverts, particularly in the intentional community where we now live, had been causing me a certain amount of stress. This stress had now been lifted.

In our village, extroverts self-select into a lot of social planning. We have a shared community building, potluck meals, pizza nights, happy hours, games nights, and parties for all sorts of occasions. A lot of the work needed to maintain our common land is done in working bees that involve considerable socialising as well as work. And beyond these community-wide activities, many of our extroverts are also groupies who prefer to do all their social, creative and exercise activities in or-ganised groups.

Rightly or wrongly, I've always felt some compulsion to join the ac-tivities of the extroverts around me. In childhood, I was told by grown-ups and teachers that it was good to work in groups and participate, that it was something I should do. Once internalised, however, this has meant a lot of searching for convincing excuses to opt out of events, or participating on the edge, waiting for a polite amount of time to elapse before feeling able to escape. Not any more! Social self-isolation has, paradoxically, freed me to enjoy being my introverted self.

Don't get me wrong. I'm not a recluse. Living with my husband, who is also my best friend, with plenty of natural environment nearby for walks, is nothing like being in full self-isolation in an urban apart-ment. We are two introverts together, which is peacefully companion-able. While we normally enjoy a modest level of social participation, having one or two friends and one or two activities on the go is enough at any given time. A full social calendar might be energising for an ex-trovert, but it is a source of stress for me.

Now, without guilt, I have more time to indulge in being rather than doing. The level of daily interruptions and distractions has gone down to the point where that magic creative zone is easier to enter and occupy for productive periods, and yet I am still in regular phone and internet contact with family. If it were not for the threat of illness and death, the present situation would be very pleasant.

I regret the lack of choice that Covid-19 has brought to our lives. We miss being able to go out to shops, galleries and restaurants; not necessarily often, but when we feel like it. I recognise the huge negative impact of Covid-19 on the lives and livelihoods of most Australians. Yes, we need to defeat it. But if and when we do, I hope, with the benefit of more self-awareness, I can somehow stop feeling like a misfit and stay true to my introvert self without guilt.

Escaping into the unknown

Borrulan laid aside his stone adze, stood and listened. There it was again – his name being called softly from among the trees. He walked towards the thicket from where his name had been called and gave a quiet whistle like that of a foraging sunbird. After a few seconds, a young woman walked softly forward from the depths of the thicket.

Borrulan took her in his arms. 'Oh Anali,' he whispered. 'I have missed you so.'

'And I you, Borrulan,' she responded, her face against his shoulder. 'I had to see you, but I can't stay long. The other women are digging roots close by and will miss me. They suspect us and watch me closely. They may even suspect I carry a forbidden child. Already my belly has begun to swell. What can we do? I am promised to the son of the chief and he grows impatient. If they guess I am bearing our forbidden child, they will kill all three of us, and I cannot hide it much longer. You said we might be able to escape from here, but where could we go? Have you thought more about it?'

Borulan led her to the small hidden clearing where he had been working. He showed her the three logs lying side by side with the cross pieces and palm matting ready to be lashed on top of them.

'See, beloved, I have a plan for us. We cannot go by land towards the sunset. All the tribes there are allies of our chief. We need to go out over the sea towards the sunrise, on the autumn winds that are now starting to blow. I am making a raft to carry us. It will look like my father's old fishing raft, but it will have secrets to help it carry us further. See, I am hollowing out the logs below the platform so the raft will ride higher and further. It will also give us a place to store warm cloaks, knives, bone awls, and the green coconuts we will need for drinking.

Since I was a small boy, I have been learning how to guide a raft for long fishing trips and find my way back to land with the help of the wind. I know how to build a shelter on a raft. I know how to use fish for food without fire, and green coconuts for water. Now it's time to use those learnings to take us far away from here to somewhere safe.'

'But Borrulan, there is no land in that direction. How will you know where to steer the raft?'

'I believe there is land out there, far out of sight towards the sunrise. Once, when father and I took his raft far out in that direction to catch yellowfish, we saw the tops of large storm clouds in that direction, the sort of clouds you see only above land. There were also birds flying in that direction. We must pray to the sea spirits that there is land there and that we can reach it. In an unknown land where no one can follow, we will be free.'

'But Borrulan, the sea is full of monsters that might kill us. I am so frightened.'

'Anali, my love, truly I am also terrified. I dream at night of storms and monsters, but none are as terrifying as the idea of us being put to death if we stay here. If we take this raft and go out towards the sunrise, at least we have a chance. I know the chief took you to the shaman to read the omens yesterday. What did he say?'

'When he laid his hand on my head, he said I would bear a strong son who would grow to be a great and wise man. But I don't dare believe him, as I think he was just trying to please the chief and the chief's son.'

'Believe him, Anali. It will help give you courage. We must believe he speaks of our son. Never forget it. Now run back to the other women before they miss you. I will finish the raft as fast as I can. When it is ready and the time is right, I will leave a red sunbird feather stuck in the bark of the coconut palm behind your hut. When you see it, come to me here in the full dark of night and we will launch the raft and go before it is light. Bring a cloak, if you can, for warmth and, if possible, some glass from the fire-mountain for making knives.'

*

And so it was that Borrulan and Anali, driven by fear of death, and a courage born of love, set out to find a new land beneath the sunrise. It was a long hard voyage with many frightening times. Fortunately, Borrulan knew how to clean the platform mats with seawater and throw fish offal far from the raft to keep circling sharks away. Though sea monsters visited at times, they were friendly, curious, and sang as they passed by.

The first land they found was just a low-lying reef covered with short scrub and seabird nests. They beached the raft and staggered out of the water half-starved and seared by sun and sea salt. But this landing gave them a chance to rest, build a driftwood fire and cook fat young birds. A diet of fat meat and fresh berries from the bushes restored their strength, but they knew, after some weeks, that they must find land with more shelter and permanent water. Land was now visible as a long dark line on the horizon to the south-east, sometimes topped with storm clouds that flickered with lightning at night. With the spirits still smiling on them, they reached this new land in time for their son to be born.

They were not the very first Australians, for a small group, escaping from massacre after a tribal war, had made the long journey before them on fishing rafts tied to each other with ropes. Shortly after their own arrival, Borrulan and Anali found these voyagers living nearby on the coast. They welcomed Borrulan and Anali as members of their group, and the women helped Anali when it came time to bear her son. True to the prophecy, their son grew into a strong and wise leader.

Getting around to it

For most of my adult life, I've been a terrible procrastinator! 'Getting around to it' has caused me all sorts of angst.

Funnily enough, it wasn't that way for everything. I was great at meeting deadlines in my job. And outside work, if I agreed to do something for someone else, I generally did it right on time. The problem was with doing things for myself, especially things involving creative expression.

In my limited free time – you know, that scrap left over when job and family had claimed their dues – I wanted to write and paint, but always struggled to get started. Often, I would sit in front of a blank sheet of paper until I ran out of time, or got sick of the problem and found some easier displacement activity. You can imagine the effect on my self-esteem!

Then one day, while browsing in a variety store, I came across a circular metal object about the size of a small dinner plate. It was brass, enamelled red with black lettering on one side:

THIS IS A ROUND TUIT.
Now that you have it, you will be able to do
all those things that have been waiting until you get a round tuit.

I couldn't resist. I had to buy it. While I didn't believe it would have magical powers, I thought it might, just possibly, psych me out of procrastination. I hung it on the wall above my desk in front of my usual vacant stare.

I put a blank sheet of paper on the desk and looked up at my tuit. 'Right, you metal marvel, tell me why I'm such a procrastinator. Then you can tell me how to get over it – simple really!'

Of course I didn't actually expect a response but, strangely, some very distinct new thoughts gradually formed in my mind.

'You're afraid of failing – of not creating anything worthwhile. You're afraid of people talking about how pathetic the result is, and how arrogant you are to even try.'

'You're afraid of being seen as selfish, doing things for yourself instead of volunteering the time to do things for others.'

'You're afraid of messing up and wasting resources – expensive paper, paints, ink – and the money they represent that could be better spent.'

Hang on a minute. Is this my tuit talking? No – it's me, definitely me – but who am I talking to? And, come to think of it, who is the 'me' who's talking?

Years ago, one of my schoolteachers tried to explain Freud's concept of id, ego, and superego. The explanation was way too premature for fourteen-year-olds and failed to produce any understanding at the time. What it did, however, was leave me with the mental picture of having another little human presence sitting inside my mind, a tiny leprechaun who could speak to me with the voices of others and hold a conversation inside my head.

It appeared my leprechaun was a nasty little character trying to hold me back from doing things I wanted to do for myself – nasty but clever – using judgemental voices to kill spontaneity.

I looked at my tuit. It hadn't actually told me anything, but something had definitely opened my mind to the issue. Now for the solution!

'OK, you brass bugger, I understand the problem. Now show me the solution.'

Unfortunately, nothing happened – that day, the next day, or for many days after that. Now I was aware of my nasty little inner leprechaun, I kept hearing the judgemental voices even more clearly. The problem seemed even worse!

But there's only so far unpleasantness can drive someone before they snap. Finally, after a particularly frustrating day, and a long sit in front of a blank sheet of paper staring at my tuit, it happened. I snapped. I sat that leprechaun down in a metaphorical corner of my mind and gave him a dressing down to curl his pointy toes:

'You miserable little stinker, how dare you tell me what others think of me! I don't care any more. Do you hear – I don't care! This is my life and I'll create what I feel like creating. I don't expect to be a famous novelist or painter. I don't expect to sell books or pictures. I'm the only important audience for my own work. If I enjoy it and it pleases me, that's enough. Do you hear – enough! Take your poison and get out of my head!'

I imagined my leprechaun leaping off his stool in fright and crawling away into a dark corner shaking in his little pointy shoes. About time!

Now I have a lot less trouble with blank sheets of paper. And my round tuit seems to be smiling a fat round smile up there on the wall.

A campfire tale

It was dusk when we pulled off the track to camp. The evening star was following the sun down in the west, while night's purple shadow was climbing into the eastern sky. We hurried to set up camp, with a ring of stones for the fire and swags laid out around it.

'Go find some firewood. Quick, before it gets dark,' said Pete, who was already rummaging in the back of the van for sausages, bread, baked beans and a frying pan.

The rest of us spread out to search for firewood in the scrub. Soon, Pete had a fire going with a pan sizzling over it, and a can of beans ready to go in on top. The wonderful smell of sausages wafted around us. It must have wafted further still. Partway through the meal, we noticed two extra figures had crept into the shady edge of our circle and sat down quietly.

'Evenin' all,' said a deep voice that stopped us all in mid-sausage. 'I'm Mikey Bilson and this is me dog Blue. Those snarlers smell awful good. Could you spare a couple for payin' guests?'

Surprised, we sat in silence for a moment to two.

Then Pete said hospitably, 'Well, I cooked a bunch of them, so I reckon we could spare a few, but you don't need to pay. Here – use my plate. I've finished. I guess Blue won't mind eating off the ground.'

'Blue and I always pay our way,' said Mikey, taking off a battered old Akubra hat and edging closer to the fire to accept a plate of food. 'I'll tell you an after-dinner yarn to pay for mine.'

He was as good as his word. When dinner was done, we relaxed around the campfire hugging mugs of billy tea while Blue paid his way by licking the plates. Finally, with the light of the campfire fading and darkness creeping over us, Mikey came good with a memorable camp-fire yarn. It went something like this.

A long time ago, when I was just a lad like you fellas, I used to saddle up the old horse and go exploring round the station after work. One time, I had my swag with me 'cause I was aiming for those hills way over there, and knew I'd have to camp overnight. After a long day crossing the plain and climbing up to the ridge, it got to be about this time of night. I'd hobbled the horse, set out my swag, eaten some bread and cheese, put the fire out, and was all set to turn in. I climbed into my swag and lay back to look at the stars – bloody beautiful they are out here with no lights around!

After a while, I began to hear, very faintly, the noise of something like chanting. It was so faint I wondered at first if I was hearing it at all. I sat up in my swag and listened hard. Gradually, the sound became clearer, as if it came from the valley on the other side of the ridge. It was strange 'cause I knew there was no one living anywhere within coo-ee in that direction. Then, in the dark of the valley, I began to make out some flickering figures dancing in circles around a fire. It could only be one thing. Somehow I was looking at a corroboree, but I had never heard of a mob living old-style anywhere near here.

After a while, I could see and hear so clearly it was pretty much like being right there in the valley. I watched the dancing and listened to the chanting for quite a while. I could even hear the stomp of dancing feet. But gradually, ever so slowly, the firelight and the dancing shadows dimmed and the sounds faded away until I could no longer hear or see anything more than just a breeze in the trees and those beautiful stars above me.

Of course I was curious to find out more about that mob in the valley so, in the morning, I packed up my camp, fetched the horse and picked my way down there. Searched all day but never found a thing, no sign of people at all – except for a few old rock drawings and some gum tree stumps with scars on them where bark had been taken off long ago! To this day, I don't know what I saw – must have been the spirits of the mob who used to live there. Maybe looking at those stars 'the right way' made me able to see and hear them.

Well, Mikey's tale sure gave us something new to think about; and when we went off to our swags, we looked at the stars a bit differently too!

Rusty

Years ago when I was growing up in Wellington, New Zealand, it was a pretty safe city by all accounts. As the pubs shut at six o'clock, night-life was almost non-existent. Young girls, however, still had a few things to worry about if they needed to go home unescorted after dark. The worries were mainly drunks turfed out of the pubs at closing time, a couple of early bikie gangs, and the very occasional older paedophile on the prowl. In my early teens, I could (and a couple of times did) run fast enough to avoid drunks and older paedophiles, but bikies? Now there's a story!

When I was sixteen, I used to go to a ballroom dancing class in town on Friday evenings. Coming from an all-girls high school, my friends and I thought this interaction with local high school boys was the pinnacle of sophisticated social activity. We even went to a local milk bar across the road for drinks after class - malted milk of course!

One Friday evening, my friend Margaret, who normally went home with me, finally enticed a much-ogled boy at the dance class to walk her home. She, I and her teenage hopeful drank a round of malted milk in the milk bar after class. They then announced they were going home together. Not wanting to cramp her style, I assured them I would be perfectly OK going home on my own. After all, it was only a three-minute walk along Wellington's main street to the foot of the local cable car (a funicular tramway) that took passengers up a steep hill into sleepy suburbia, where another short five-minute walk would take me to my home. What could go wrong!

When I arrived at the entry to Cable-Car Lane, however, I found with some horror a small gathering of local bikies, who had parked about eight bikes in the entry and were hanging out in a playful mood.

As I started to weave my way between the bikes, I was hassled with suggestive comments, pats on the bottom and a few attempts to grope higher up. Then my path was blocked by several leathered and tattooed bodies and a fairly aggressive suggestion that I should climb on the back of one of the bikes to have some fun on the way home. As you can imagine, I was getting alarmed at this point but, fortunately, help was at hand.

Straddled across the pillion seat of one of the bikes was a tall boy dressed in a duffel coat rather than bikie regalia, who looked to be not too much older than me. He climbed off the bike and came over saying, 'I'll take you home,' which triggered a lot of bawdy joking and laughter from the main bikie group.

So I had to decide on the spot whether to wait for possible help from the empty street, carry on trying to defy the bikie group, or accept a walk home with one of them. I looked up at him, trying to make up my mind. I had no idea if or when another passer-by might come along who could rescue me. Certainly, the odds were better with one boy on foot than about eight or so on motorbikes.

So I took a gamble and accepted his offer to walk me home.

He put his arm around my shoulders, pulled me close against him, and we strolled off to the cable car entrance, followed by bawdy comments and much laughter.

As soon as we were through the entrance and out of sight of the group, he stopped, took his arm off my shoulders, turned to me and said, 'Hello. I'm Rusty. Sorry to get personal like that but I had to make my brother and his mates think I was going to score. They're only interested in one thing at the moment and you don't look like that sort of girl. Hold my hand so people will just think you're my girlfriend.'

My gamble had paid off. Here, in very unlikely company, was a perfect young duffel-coated gentleman. He paid my cable car fare in spite of my protest that I should pay for myself, and walked me right to my front gate. We chatted on the way, almost like established friends, and he suggested, just like a real big brother, that I really shouldn't walk around on my own after dark, even in a quiet city like Wellington. He even gave me a quick peck on the cheek when he said goodnight and walked away.

He was obviously a cut above most of the gauche teenage talent I had encountered at that time but, somewhat to my regret, I never saw him again.

A question of good or bad

Some years ago, as concerns grew about the environment, persistent plastics became an increasing worry. There were campaigns to get rid of disposable coffee cups and single-use plastic packaging. There were calls to remove plastic bags from aquatic food chains. And there were volunteer drives to generally 'Clean up Australia'.

We were shown shocking images of dead seabirds with stomachs full of plastic, turtles choked by straws and plastic film, huge areas of floating plastic garbage in ocean gyres, and even a plastic bag eleven kilometres down in the Marianas Trench. China no longer accepted our plastic waste for recycling, and we had no satisfactory answers of our own.

In spite of all the hand wringing, it seemed we were collectively deaf, wedded to convenience technologies and unwilling to give them up.

It was at this point that Barrie, a fellow student in my molecular genetics course, took up the environmental cause. He selected an insanely ambitious research topic for his PhD: 'Genetic engineering of soil and water microbes to degrade plastic polymers'.

Most of us had been encouraged by our supervisors to choose topics for which results were readily achievable if existing technical protocols were followed. Barrie's project, however, had no existing protocols, and the chance of any result seemed vanishingly small. The rest of us thought he was crazy.

Needless to say, Barrie was still conscientiously working on his research when the rest of the class had graduated and gone to find jobs. We looked on what he was attempting as a sad joke.

'Poor old Barrie! He's never going to crack it in a hundred years. About the only thing he's ever going to achieve is a bug we can load into his coffin to compost him quickly!'

Well, believe it or not, Barrie finally had the last laugh. Some four years after the rest of us had graduated, a brief article in the local newspaper gave a hint of his progress. The headline read, 'Local researcher wins CalTech scholarship!' Barrie had sparked international interest with an engineered bacterium that could rapidly break down two common polymers. The research was of sufficient interest to earn a major research grant and access to a fully staffed laboratory.

There was no further news for several more years, but then a new article caught my eye, with a photo of Barrie, older but still as scruffy as ever, and a headline saying, 'Researcher blasts ocean garbage'. The photo showed Barrie leaning out of a motor launch, spraying the Pacific garbage gyre with liquid from a large hose.

There was initial interest, of course, but it took another couple of years before reports began to acknowledge the success of the project. By then, measurements from the space station showed, beyond a doubt, that the garbage patch was shrinking.

Problem solved? Well, not really. The plastic-eating bacteria were, as you might expect, gradually dispersed throughout the world's oceans and subsequently into land-based freshwater systems. They were small enough to be taken up off the ocean surface by wind and then fall to earth in rain. Most plastics, especially plastic bags, vanished rapidly from waterways and hopes were high that plastic pollution had been dealt with.

But then along came the law of unintended consequences to spoil the party. Clothes made from polymers such as polyester and nylon began rotting in wardrobes and off people's backs. Polyester insulation began to vanish out of walls and ceilings. Curtains fell in rags from windows. All sorts of household and industrial equipment, including computers, TVs, and even cars, began to degrade at unprecedented rates. PVC, while slower to break down because of inherent toxicity, eventually began to degrade with very unpleasant results for domestic sewerage systems.

Suddenly, it seemed, everyone was arguing the merits or otherwise of the new plastic-eating bacteria. Were they good or were they bad?

And were plastics themselves good or bad? Barrie, who had been lauded as a heroic genius, was now being demonised by some as the man who wrecked modern life and destroyed all the valuable, durable products of polymer science.

Plastic-eating bacteria were novel technology, very different from anything that went before. They were alive, 'out there', and reproducing. The genie could not be put back in the bottle!

In future, plastics would need to be used differently – perhaps similarly to the way wood is used in the presence of natural wood-rotting fungi and bacteria.

As the argument wound down, it was concluded that plastics were similar to coal, oil and other technologies: They were not, in themselves, inherently bad, but problems arose from the way they were used and abused by society. So again we have to conclude that whether a technology is good or bad actually depends on whether we can trust humans with it or not!

It's the size of the page that matters

Richard is tall, with an angular face and tousled, sandy hair. His slim build is emphasised by his favourite style of dress – narrow black jeans and a turtleneck sweater. When you talk to him, it quickly becomes clear that he is deeply fascinated by the natural world. Curiosity, respect and concern for the environment are a part of his every waking moment, and almost every conversation. Many find him exciting to talk to, but those whose primary concerns are with politics and economics find him tiring and often confronting. In many ways, he is a man of his background – a long line of frugal, academic Scots for whom the wild beauty of their highland landscape was long revered as nothing short of sacred.

Tina, on the other hand, comes from a large, close-knit, southern Italian family. The daily activities of the many members, including dozens of cousins and bambini, have always been of consuming interest through the generations. Birthdays are generously celebrated, likes and dislikes well known; hopes and dreams widely discussed. Tina and her family love nothing so much as a large family occasion, full of animated conversation and mountains of good food.

Tina is short in stature. Some might initially call her dumpy but after a second look, this description soon gives way to something much kinder – like curvaceous or lush. She has masses of wavy black hair and large, expressive dark eyes. Her smile is a permanent feature – a joyful acceptance of everyone she meets. Somehow, without seeming to pry, she quickly manages to find out how old someone is, where they come from, what they do for a living and what they intend to do with their life. People talk to her easily and enjoy the encounter. She is a people person through and through, with a vital interest in social systems and how they might promote a more equitable, humane society.

How on earth did two such dissimilar individuals come together as a couple? Aha – therein lies a story.

They first met as members of the student debating society. Richard's entry to university was expected in light of family tradition. Tina, however, was the first person in her family to attempt tertiary studies. With passionate viewpoints and a love of discussion, it was natural that these two were drawn to the ideological jousting of formal debates.

For the first year of overlapping membership, they took part in different debating areas – environmental issues for Richard, and social justice systems for Tina. While they were certainly aware of each other in a physical sense, they were on totally different pages intellectually. Although liking the look of each other, they simply couldn't abide each other's world view.

Over the following year, the society began to bring issues of environment, poverty and social justice together in broader-ranging debates on sustainability. Now, Richard and Tina often found themselves in direct ideological conflict on opposing teams in the same debate. Both were eloquent speakers who gained recognition for their ability to present and often clinch a line of reasoning. They both experienced winning and losing, but there was one debate that became famous throughout the campus for their utterly unexpected standout performance.

Picture it: Richard has just presented his reasoning for why environmental integrity is fundamental to sustainability of the whole earth system, referring in the course of his argument to the human population as a plague and cities as cancers on the Earth.

Tina is furious. This goes against some of her deepest humanist feelings. She refuses, however, to give in easily. In summing up for her team, she is devastating. She coolly outlines a compelling pair of possible futures, one a socially just system that encourages better lives along with environmental respect, and one in which coercive attempts to preserve wild nature create an unsupportive home for impoverished humanity.

Richard is desperate to stop this clearly winning rhetoric. Over the year, his respect for Tina's intellect has grown, and he has a sneaking appreciation (not yet overtly acknowledged) for her point of view. How can he stop this rout?

He stands, walks over to Tina at the microphone, grabs her and stops that devastating stream of logic with a kiss. And what a kiss; it's worthy of the best movie love scenes! It goes on and on. The audience, after an initial gasp of surprise, begins to whistle, cheer and stamp.

Eventually, the debate adjudicator gets up, walks over, and taps Richard on the shoulder. 'Excuse me,' he says, 'we're declaring a draw. Both teams have clearly finished up on the same page. The page just got larger!'

Richard and Tina step back from each other, panting, their eyes wide with astonishment. Tina grabs Richard's hand and tows him out of the hall while the audience settles down and things get back on track. When next seen, Richard and Tina are still holding hands.

They have been on the same larger page ever since.

Saved by the rats of the sea

I stood on the cliff, leaning into a wind that threatened to tear the coat from my shoulders. Gulls soared and swooped in the turbulent mist rising up from the surf, their cries in harmony with the desolate landscape. Far below, I could see the narrow ledges where their sparse nests clung precariously. It had taken several hours to reach the gull rookery, walking along the cliff from my holiday shack. But the scudding dark clouds now trailed grey curtains of rain. It was time to return.

As I turned, I stumbled on a loose rock, staggering as I tried to regain my balance. With a shock of horror, I felt the cliff edge around me give way. Then I was falling – falling down towards the pounding surf, my head bumping over rocks in a cascade of rattling pebbles. The world went dark and I felt nothing more.

At some point, I became aware of a world of pain – lancing, throbbing, screaming through my mind, but perhaps the screaming was only the wind or the gulls. There was no light, but I could sense solid ground beneath me. I seemed to be lying on something hard, cold and damp. It was enough for now to know I was alive. The dark of night was no time for sorting out the pain, so I lay still.

When I next became conscious, it was light and I could see gulls swooping above me. Carefully I reached out and explored the ground around me. I was sprawled on a narrow ledge with several gulls' nests beside me under a rocky overhang. My head and one ankle throbbed with pain. I licked the wet rock to slake my thirst, but it was sea spray and too salty to swallow.

Reality began to dawn on me. I was in a remote wilderness, miles from anywhere, and no one had any reason to look for me. After spending much of the last twenty-four hours unconscious, wet and cold, I was still in too much pain to try climbing up or down the cliff. Unless I could somehow get moving and rescue myself, there was a good chance I could die of hunger, thirst, and exposure.

Slowly, painfully, with infinite care to avoid falling off my rocky ledge, I moved into a sitting position with my back to the cliff. Normally, I am a confident rock climber, but in this state, with what seemed to be a sprained ankle and possible concussion, I was weaker than the proverbial kitten and suffering badly from thirst and hunger.

I sat and thought about what I could possibly drink or eat. The rain had stopped, so there was no fresh water running down the cliff. The few meagre tufts of grass at one end of the ledge wouldn't keep a goat alive for five minutes. I looked at the grey speckled eggs in the gull nests that shared my ledge. Were they still just eggs, or did they contain chicks about to hatch? It was not an appealing thought but I was getting desperate.

As the parent birds screamed and swooped, I edged along to the first nest, picked up an egg and held it up to the light. It seemed dark and lumpy inside. Was that a chick? I put it back, moved to the next nest and tried again. This time the egg looked uniform inside, so I gently cracked one end against the cliff and lifted off a cap of shell. There was no sign of a chick in this one, just the white and yolk of a new egg. Gratefully, I lifted it to my open mouth and let it slide in.

Normally, I would find a raw egg slimy and revolting to eat. This one, however, was just about the best thing I had ever tasted. It was wonderfully smooth, moist, slightly salty, and satisfying on my parched tongue – a little survival package of food and drink together. Quickly, I finished off the remaining two eggs in the nest and lay down to rest again.

By the following morning, I felt a lot better and, after raiding another couple of nests, managed to crawl around the cliff from the ledge to a small, steep gully leading up to the cliff top. It took a long time to crawl up it, and all the rest of the day to limp home, but I made it.

Seagulls get a bad rap as 'rats of the sea' but now I am always glad to see them. I owe them a lot – maybe even my life!

Time will fix everything

Arnu wipes his slippery hands on the grass. The stench of the midden behind the huts is gut-churning after a day in the sun. He tosses the fish bones and clamshells from the family meal up onto the stinking heap and walks quickly away. Returning to the cooking area, he helps his mother put the fire out by kicking earth over it. Then he picks up his spear and jogs down to the creek to find his friends before sunset. Some are splashing in the swimming hole, while a couple are keeping watch. Alligators, wolves and hostile strangers all need to be avoided.

Calling to his friend Bailu, Arnu swings into the pool from a low branch, landing with a splash that soaks the whole group. As the water closes over him, he doubles over and swims along the bottom to find Bailu. A pair of brown legs appears out of the murk in front of him. Quickly, he grabs the ankles and lifts up and over. There is a loud yell of fright and a satisfying splash. Laughing, he comes to the surface, flicking water from his hair. Bailu is floundering noisily, trying to regain his balance. He is not happy to have been tossed off his feet, mainly because he feels tricked by his own first thought – that he had been grabbed by an alligator.

As the boys around them gradually head home, the two friends wrestle in the water for a while, removing dirt, sweat and fish slime in the process. With the sun now setting behind the dunes, they climb out of the water, plucking their spears out of the earth on the way.

Bailu turns towards the pool for a last look at the rippling reflections of red sky. 'Arnu,' he calls excitedly, 'there's a big fish in the pool. I just saw its shadow in the water.' Not waiting for a response, he grabs his spear, runs down the bank and leaps into the water.

Arnu sees his spear break the surface, then his head, yelling wildly as the water thrashes and foams around him. Arnu runs to the edge of the pool looking for a way to help, but darkness is falling and he can't see well enough. Helplessly, he stands on the bank as the commotion gradually dies down and the surface of the pool becomes empty and still. The silence is frightening.

He races to the huts for help. The men follow him back to the creek at a run; but the night is now black and silent and nothing can be seen. They call Bailu's name for a long time, eventually falling silent when there is no response. The rising moon reveals the surface of the pool as a motionless silver mirror.

Arnu's father puts one arm around Arnu and the other around Bailu's father, who is weeping silently. 'Come home,' he says, 'there is nothing we can do in the dark. We'll come back tomorrow as soon as it's light.'

With shoulders drooping and tears falling, the little group returns to the huts; but no one sleeps that night.

At first light, the menfolk and boys go back to the creek. The sight that greets them is horrifying. Bailu floats among the reeds, his body a mass of torn flesh. Near him floats a large alligator with Bailu's spear lodged deep in its neck. Both are dead.

Silent in their grief, they pull both bodies from the water, bind them to spears, and carry them back to the huts where the womenfolk set up a great wailing.

Later in the day, the shaman quiets the wailing and prepares to send Bailu to the spirit world. 'Bailu, you die a warrior. You will be buried with a necklace of teeth from your alligator, so the spirits you encounter will know you as a mighty hunter. To honour your hunting, we will dine on your kill until only the bones remain. Then we will go from here, back to the winter hunting grounds, to give your spirit time to find its place, free from the mourning voices of the people. Arnu, you have lost your friend, but remember that time will fix everything. Bailu's spirit will be here to protect you when we return next summer.'

So Arnu dries his tears and, in the name of friendship, calls on the spirit of Bailu to guard him for a lifetime from the menace of dark waters.

When the tribe returns the following summer, the sun-bleached alligator bones are scattered on a midden that no longer smells of rotting flesh. All summer, Arnu feels the powerful presence of Bailu's spirit, guiding his spear and calling the biggest fish to swim into his net.

Adventure within

When you suggested I write about an adventure, my first reaction was to think of a physical adventure. You know – something to do with an exciting or dangerous encounter, exploring in the outback, touring foreign countries, an extreme moment in sport, and so forth.

I've had a few of these adventures over the years, but when I imagined writing a description of any of them, they seemed to pale into insignificance beside *intellectual* adventures – adventures of the mind. Looking back, I can see this different type of adventure has meant more in my life than physical adventure. I suspect many people wouldn't think of these intellectual experiences as adventures, and it took me years to recognise them this way.

We all love to be regaled with stories about physical adventures. The news is full of them. Authors invent them for us. They occupy many shelves in libraries. They tell us about the sorts of doings and happenings, real or imagined, that anyone can relate to – but what of intellectual adventures?

Think of the old story of Archimedes in his bath, puzzling over how to tell whether a king's golden crown was adulterated with silver. His intellectual discovery about density and displacement of water was so exciting he leapt out of the bath and ran naked through the city shouting, 'Eureka! I've got it.' Now, that's an intellectual adventure!

This is what scientists mean when they talk reverently about eureka moments, moments when pieces of a scientific mystery click into place in the mind, so that all the connections and implications suddenly become clear, logical and comprehensible.

Imagine how amazing it feels to know you have discovered something that no one else knows – not one single other member of humanity. It may be only something small. It may never be worth a Nobel Prize. It may not have a lot of relevance in the main stream of today's society; but the sheer fact of its unique discovery is like a tiny bubble of pleasure – a fabulous feeling of achievement. Even if you explain it to someone who then yawns and says, 'So what!' it is still your adventure, and their failure to comprehend it or feel the magic is their loss, not yours.

With the right teachers, children can experience moments like this during their education. They depend on the child's own curiosity and a learning environment that fosters it, rather than suppressing it under syllabus strictures and formal lessons – a bureaucratic recipe that risks educating creative minds to oblivion! Exceptional teachers can catalyse adventures of the mind; explaining something in such a way that a receptive young person can 'see' and 'feel' how it works – a type of deep, unforgettable comprehension that helps make sense out of so much more beyond the original puzzle. I was lucky enough to have two such teachers during my education. They put excitement into my life, gave me a lifetime career, and prepared me for the ultimate personal adventure of new discovery.

Twice I've had a personal eureka adventure – the discovery of something totally unknown before I came along. Not Nobel Prize stuff; not the winning goal of a world cup; not reaching the summit of Everest; probably of interest only to scientists in my own field; but what a profound sense of achievement. Knowing I had seen something that was undiscovered by generations of others. Knowing I had lifted the lid on another of Nature's secrets. What a buzz!

The bush or the sea

'It's a lovely house, Susie dear,' said Mother subsiding into the sofa after a tour of Susan and Bernie's new home. 'I do like these lovely aqua floor tiles and the beautiful natural timber floor in the hallway. The bathroom and kitchen are nice too, and they'll be easy to keep clean. You have done well for yourselves.'

'Thanks, Mum,' said Susan. 'We're very happy with it. We got it for a reasonable price too, considering the ocean views. Would you like a cup of tea? I have your favourite tea in the pot and some fresh scones.' She gestured towards the afternoon tea spread on the table in front of them.

'Thank you, dear. I would love a cup of tea, and fresh scones too. You do know how to tempt me.'

As Susan poured tea and served the scones with jam and cream, her mother continued. 'The ocean view is lovely, but what will you do about the garden? The shrubs on the slope below the deck are blown flat against the hill. Perhaps it's just as well there are no trees. They could be dangerous in the sort of gales you must get here on the coast.'

She took a sip of tea and continued, 'Where will you grow your flowers and vegies? We've always had a garden full of flowers and vegies at home. Surely you'll miss them if you have nowhere flat or sheltered to grow things away from the salty winds. And what about the bush and the gum trees. Won't you miss having them around you? For me they have always been like a nice green, sheltering cocoon to come home to, and such a nice backdrop for the flower beds.'

Susan took a scone and topped it will jam and cream before answering. 'Honestly, Mum, in the three months since we moved in, we haven't even thought about trying to grow flowers and vegies. If we ever did, we might need to put in a little courtyard or glasshouse on the east where there's a bit of shelter. When we bought the house, we chose it for the house itself, of course, but also the wonderful sea views.'

She gestured to the large windows lining two walls of the living room overlooking the gulf. 'I never get sick of looking at that huge sea and sky in all sorts of weathers. The light and the colours are amazing – blues, greens, greys, and white – changing all the time with the wind and clouds. The sunsets are fabulous too, and you wouldn't believe all the stars in the night sky. I feel as though I want to capture every different moment. The views have taken me back to my old hobby of painting, and I'm really enjoying it. Bernie has even gone back to photography. He's been taking photos of sea, sunsets and wild weather.'

'That's nice, dear,' said mother, pouring herself a second cup of tea and selecting another scone. 'But I can't help wondering whether you might get tired of all the wind and weather after a while. Remember that discussion we had a few years ago when you first got engaged? The offer still stands.'

Susan mentally took a deep breath. She could guess what was coming next.

Her mother dealt with a bite of scone and then continued. 'The bush block at the end of the garden is still there if you want it someday. You could clear a few trees and build something nice there. Or, if I'm getting past doing the garden by then, perhaps you could even take over the existing house and garden. I could always have a nice little cabin built for me among the trees on the back block. That way, I could still enjoy the main gardens. There are plenty of vegies for us all, and flowers for both houses too.'

Susan poured herself another tea to give herself space to think. How could she make mother understand her fear of being surrounded by trees when these same trees were the sheltering cocoon her mother loved so much?

'Thanks, Mum. That's a wonderful offer and we appreciate it, really we do, but we're both open sky people. We need vistas rather than close-in views. And after this last summer, I would be much too afraid of fire to ever go back to living it the bush. It was great when I was a kid, but the climate has changed so much since then. Fire would be a constant worry. I was actually quite worried about you living among trees over this past summer. Wouldn't you prefer to move to a nice little retirement unit in town?'

Mother gave a shudder. 'Oh no, dear, I would hate leaving my home. Maybe it's best we all go on as we are for a while. Have you met your neighbours yet? What are they like?'

The mysterious guardians

They say one picture is worth a thousand words, but I have in mind a picture that could be worth many stories and several thousand words at least. It was on the cover of a volume of science fiction short stories borrowed years ago from the library.

I picked the book off the shelf because the cover picture so intrigued me, but in none of the stories within the book was it explained. Perhaps, partly as a result, it thoroughly captured my imagination. Even now, years later, it lurks there in my mind, fascinating and tantalising, but I remain forever the mystified outside observer.

Looking from the sea towards a rocky shore, the impression is one of impending darkness, almost of sorrow, of magnificence departed and a long night about to fall. Perhaps the French word *tristesse* captures it best. The observer is looking against the sun, sunk low behind tall, dark, craggy, coastal cliffs. Its direct rays still reach and colour a few clouds overhead at the top of the picture.

A narrow line of rocky beach at the foot of the cliffs, closer on the right and fading away into the distance on the left, is already in shadow, except for a slim beam of sunlight lingering in the middle distance where a stream gully cuts the cliff to the base. Somehow, I know the sun is setting, not rising, but is this on our world or another?

While the landscape might seem unremarkable for anyone who grew up near an east-facing rocky shore, an otherworldly sense of mystery emanates from a row of six gigantic white stone statues like crouching lions or griffons, their feet in the breaking waves, at intervals along the beach. Further along the coast, the line of statues recedes into a distant haze of surf mist suggesting, with its wraiths and shadows, that there are many more of them. Are they guardians of the land?

They are monstrously old, not of today. The cracks and scars of age are clearly seen on the nearest, and further along the line, at least two are ravaged and broken, their great stone blocks, heads or limbs, lying in the surf around their bases. They speak silently of greatness, of strength and power now departed, of some vanished people, great artisans, masters of technology and spiritual achievement, gone but not quite vanished into oblivion.

For the observer, the most compelling and mysterious part of the picture is two small childish figures, a young boy and girl, golden-haired, dressed in plain short, Grecian-style tunics, belted with gold at the waist and arrestingly white against the deep shadow of the cliffs behind them. The boy has climbed the nearest statue, many times taller than he is, and stands proudly on its head, feet braced apart, tunic flared by the wind, pointing with one outstretched arm across the sea beyond the picture. What is he pointing at? Approaching night, a rising moon, perhaps more than one moon, a sea monster rising from the water, a ship of some kind, a great invasion? The girl stands beside the statue, feet in the edge of the water, looking up at him with one arm reaching up as if pleading for a hand to help her up to see.

Who are they? Where are the others, their parents and people? Are they gone? Are these children the last of a vanished race or, like the phoenix rising from the ashes, the first inhabitants of a new brighter future? The mystery seems to demand an explanation. Even after all this time, the picture still sits in my mind. I hunger to know the story in the mind of the artist. It is so tantalising that nowhere in the book was the picture explained or the story told.

Grudgingly, however, I acknowledge the artist as a science fiction writer no less than the authors of the stories in the book. The picture sets the scene for many stories of its own. Perhaps I am just lazily resentful that I have to imagine them for myself!

The man in the bowler hat

Early twentieth century

I remember my first day of work as though it were yesterday. I was a cheeky rascal, accustomed to an easy life playing in the streets of east London. My dad was a dock worker earning just enough to keep a family of four fed and clothed. It was a matter of pride to him in those days that Mother didn't need to go out to work as well.

On my fourteenth birthday, my father sat me down for a serious talk about life's responsibilities. 'Well, lad,' he said, 'you've learned enough now about reading and arithmetic. It's time to leave school, stop running around the streets, and start helping to support the family. You need a job, and I know a good man who might help you get a start. Tomorrow, you'll come to the docks with me and see Mr Bailey about an apprenticeship in his ships chandlers business.'

Well, believe me; I was less cocky about life the next morning. Dad woke me up before it was light. We had a quick breakfast together before setting off for the docks. When we reached Bailey's warehouse, we went through a big glass door to the polished wooden counter inside. Dad took off his cap to introduce me to the clerk. I quickly took off my own cap and shook hands just as Dad had taught me.

'I'm here to see Mr Bailey about a job,' I explained.

The clerk grinned. I'm sure he could tell I was nervous.

'Yes, I think he'll be expecting you,' said the clerk. 'Follow me.' He lifted a section of the counter for me to pass through.

''Bye, son,' said Dad. 'I'll see you when I get home from work.' He turned and went out through the door, putting his cap on as he went.

The clerk took me down a back corridor to a door with a polished brass nameplate – *E.H. Bailey – General Manager*.

'Wait here,' he said. 'Mr Bailey will be in directly. He'll see you as soon as he arrives.'

I'll never forget my first sight of Mr Bailey coming down the corridor. He was a very tall, lean man with a high bowler hat that made him look even taller. He had a long face and long, straight nose. His cheeks were clean-shaven, but he had a neatly trimmed beard on his chin and a few traces of grey amongst the red-brown of his hair and beard.

'Hello, lad,' he said. 'So you'd like to join the ships chandlers business. Come on in and we can talk about it.'

He opened the door and I followed. As he hung up his coat and hat on the coat stand inside, I noticed his hands. They we not like my dad's strong labouring hands with their rough skin. They were white with long elegant fingers. He had a ring on his left hand that matched the fancy cufflinks in his sleeves. I thought I'd like to have hands like that one day

'Sit down, lad,' he said, indicating a chair in front of a large mahogany desk.

I sat down nervously, cap in hand. Mr Bailey sat down in a big leather chair behind the desk and leant forward on his elbows. His calm, interested expression helped me feel less nervous as he slowly led me through some questions about myself, my schoolwork, and my hopes for the future.

Finally, he leant back and smiled kindly. 'Well, lad, reckon I like what I hear, so the apprenticeship's yours. Now I'll take you to Mr Fenton, our master of stores. He'll be your first supervisor. This business is all about well-run stores, so the main storeroom is where you'll start.'

Well, you wouldn't have known it from the way I meekly followed Mr Bailey out of the office but, inside my mind, I was hopping up and down with glee. 'I've got a job. I've got a job.' I couldn't wait to tell my dad.

So that was the start of it all, and I can honestly say I loved every minute of working for Mr Bailey. He ran a strict but fair workplace, and we all knew that he himself, while outwardly stern, cared for us all in a way that many bosses of the time did not. Nobody willingly gave up a job at Baileys.

Now, many years later, the brass plate on the managing director's door carries my name – but I'll never forget Mr Bailey. We should all be so lucky to start out in a job the way I did.

'Home' and 'Place'

'Home' and 'my place' are two expressions that seem to be used interchangeably, but are they always saying the same thing?

Home, for me, is the house in which I live with my husband in the Aldinga Arts EcoVillage. It's an eco-home that cocoons the two of us comfortably, smoothing out seasonal temperature fluctuations; sheltering us from hot dusty winds in summer and the cold gales of winter. It guards our financial security by removing the need to pay for water, electricity, sewerage services, petrol and some of our food. The compact, intentional community around us contributes friends, a range of shared social and arts activities, opportunities for volunteering, chances to join in cooperative projects, car sharing, pet sharing, repurposing of surplus stuff by neighbours, and the security of many eyes watching everything, day and night.

Home is therefore a term that evokes love, companionship, comfort, belonging and safety.

On the other hand, the term 'my place' is complex, elusive and deeply entwined with intense feelings and memories. Superficially, my place is the one room in our home reserved for my own personal activities like writing and painting.

At a deeper level, however, my place is a much bigger and more nebulous concept – probably akin to the Indigenous sense of country. In my deepest consciousness, my place has broad ocean views, windswept sand dunes, breaking waves, long beaches, tidal rock pools, driftwood along the tidelines, and the sound of seagulls riding strong, cold winds. It has steep green hillsides covered with dense, wind-ruffled forest and bushland. There are cool, moist valleys sheltering ancient ferns and mosses beside shady streams that tumble steeply down to the sea. The bush is penetrated only by steep, narrow foot tracks and occasional shady unsealed roads in the valley bottoms.

Strangely perhaps, my place also has wide, red, desert landscapes where the bones of the land show through a meagre covering of plants, and all living things yearn for water. Here I can stand on a railway track, the only man-made feature in a flat 360-degree landscape, and see the track vanish into a distant point on the horizon to both the east and west. The high point in this landscape is a lone tree, stark and dead, its few remaining bare branches reaching into the upturned bowl of hard blue waterless sky, pleading for the rain that used to fall when it was young.

But above all, my place is empty of crowds. It is an introvert's paradise filled with quiet places to sit and absorb unspoilt views and sounds of nature. There are family members and companions here also, but our interactions are by choice rather than social necessity, and there are plenty of spaces in our friendships and togetherness.

My place is not digitally connected. It is real, not virtual. Its human interactions are person to person and its sweeping views are different from minute to minute rather than captured forever on a screen. It experiences time at a slow, natural pace, with no noisy, polluting traffic, and no unwanted music, radio voices, telephones or social media. In my place, the main voices are those of the sea, the wind and the birds. This is a place that presents possibilities for art, poetry and literature, but never demands them. They seem to emerge naturally and gently from Nature and solitude.

An encounter with my place can tap into intense emotions quite distinct from the comfortable love of home. The primeval beauty of my place sometimes moves me to tears and a feeling of profound attachment akin to joy. But I can also be moved to tears of sorrow or rage when I see it suffering from careless human damage, exploitation and so-called development. These days, I am often satisfied by the knowledge that my place still exists rather than feeling the compulsion to walk into it myself and contribute further to its human burden.

How can these concepts of home and place be so divergent? Is my inner nature in conflict with outward reality? Are there two separate universes inside my mind? I think perhaps there are.

Home relates to the daily environment, with its everyday comfortable relationships, and the reality of living in the present. My place, however, is built from memories, from all the accumulated peak experiences of a loner with a reverence for Nature, and from concern about growing human impacts. My psyche emerges from both these universes; both enrich me and, if I were to lose either one, I would be greatly impoverished.

Word games

I was brought up in the best British tradition to be very superior. After all, an *Oxford Dictionary* is no ordinary book. Even a *Pocket Oxford* like me has prestigious, well-bred credentials.

For years, I sat on the desk of a serious student of English who used to go through the morning and evening newspapers and comment, via letters to the editors, on errors of spelling, grammar and misuse of words. Although he never heard back from the editors, I'm sure his reports, made with my help and careful citations, were much valued in their offices.

In those days, my favourite word was onomatopoeia – the word which describes other words that sound like what they mean – crash or sizzle, for example. It used to amuse me to fall open on the desk at a page containing an onomatopoetic word. He and I used to have good discussions of whether certain words were actually onomatopoeic or not.

One day, however, my serious student moved on in his life, and I found myself in a cluttered, dusty, second-hand bookshop. I had trouble coming to terms with being sold for only a tenth of my new price, and was quite depressed about it for a while. The change, however, eventually turned out to be amazingly positive. After many weeks of being picked up, put down and thumbed over, someone bought me and wrapped me up with a Scrabble set as a present for a young girl.

What a partner that Scrabble set turned out to be. We both loved words, but learning to work together took at little while. When I introduced my favourite word, onomatopoeia, the Scrabble set was unimpressed: 'Too long and not enough high-value letters!'

Well, I got the message and worked hard at learning the values of the various little letter tiles. We began to present our owner with winning words such as 'query' (17), 'blaze' (16), and 'zephyr' (23). What a team. I was still good at falling open at particular pages, so now I concentrated on pages containing high-value words; and my Scrabble partner was quite skilled at causing the most interesting combinations of tiles to be picked by chance. Together we fostered our owner as a Scrabble champion throughout her schooldays and beyond.

Now, although we are both back on the bookshelf again, we are there together, with lots of words to discuss, and the hope that those two little children playing with their toys on the rug beside the bookshelf will eventually grow up and put us to work again.

The herbalist

Thirteenth-century England

'Everything,' said Sister Rachel, seating herself on a bench in the sun, 'begins with the plants God created. They give us food. They give us medicines. And they provide for all of God's creatures as well. How blessed we are by such a bounty all around us.' She settled herself more comfortably, smoothed the black skirts of her habit, and looked out across the neat rows of plants.

I sat quietly, respectfully, the newest of the abbey's postulants, thirteen years old, and directed just this morning by Mother Superior to assist Sister Rachel in the herb garden.

'You will need to pay attention, young Elizabeth,' said Sister Rachel, glancing my way with a serious expression. 'There is a lot to learn. You need to know how to grow all the herbs you can see here in the garden, as well as how to dry and preserve them. Then you will need to know how to make herbal tonics and remedies from them, and how to use them to heal the sick and keep us healthy. It will take many years before you can take over growing and using the garden. It's what Mother Superior desires you to do in time, and I won't be here forever to guide you.'

She crossed herself and continued, 'One day God will call me, and then you must be prepared. You will need to know everything I know and more besides if you are to become the abbey herbalist after I go. Well, no time like the present. Let's start with the bees. Come with me.'

She stood up and led the way to a group of wicker beehives against the fence in a corner of the garden. Bees were busily flying in and out.

'Bees,' she told me, 'are our best workers in the garden. If they don't visit the flowers, no seeds or fruit will set. And besides that, the honey they make is one of the best dressings for wounds. You always need bee-hives close to the garden. Their doorway should face the east and, once the sun is up, there should always be bees going in and out. If you can't see bees, that means trouble.'

As we watched the bees, she pointed out the little pollen baskets on their back legs. 'See there, Elizabeth, that's how the bees take payment for their work, with nectar and pollen to feed their young in the hive.'

So that was how my training began. Every day, I followed Sister Rachel around the garden learning about the plants and their uses. I helped in the big fragrant workroom where harvested herbs were sorted and hung in bunches from the rafters to dry. Then, when the weather was inclement, she taught me how to use the big stone mortar to grind dried herbs, and how to use hot water, oils or brandy to extract herbal essences and make fragrant lotions.

Everything we made had to be stored in glass or pottery jars and carefully labelled, so I was glad I had learned my letters well in the schoolroom. I took a pride in my neat labels. Some herbs like belladonna, foxglove and henbane could be deadly if used wrongly, so it was very important to label them correctly and put them on a special high shelf in the storeroom.

I'll never forget the first time I went with Sister Rachel to the infirmary to treat one of our sisters who was sick with the ague and shaking terribly with fever. I watched as Sister Rachel gently questioned her about her symptoms and then gave her a cup of hot willow-bark tea. She left instructions for the infirmary sister to repeat this twice a day until the ague was gone.

I loved my work in the garden. It was peaceful and felt close to God's wisdom. Sister Rachel was a patient, kind teacher, and so gentle when she treated the sick. I grew to respect and love her more over time. For the first three seasons, I followed her closely and was supervised in everything I did. But as the fourth season began and I prepared to take my final vows, she gave me half the garden and half the beehives to manage on my own. She also began to give me responsibility for preparing some of the medicines. In that year also, I made my first unsupervised trip to the infirmary to treat a sister who had been burned while turning the spit in the kitchen.

By the end of the sixth season, my confidence and knowledge of the herbalist's role had grown. I felt my spirit becoming one with this important part of God's work. As it became my own life's work, I was blessed with peace and fulfilment.

A life: eternal, universal?

'That's strange,' said Jai Peros looking at the image of planet Marta in the FarViewer. 'There's a dark area that wasn't there last year. I wonder what it is. Usually the surface is red but that small patch might have a hint of green. Here, have a look. What do you think?' She moved aside for Canove Singun.

After staring for some time, he said, 'I think you might be right. Let's take a hi-res image of the surface in tru-color.'

After taking the image, they made a note of their unusual observation, and stored both in the annual survey of near-Earta planets. They then moved to other tasks. As members of Solar System Survey, their job was to record and image the surfaces of these planets every year.

The next year, Jai noted that the mysterious patch was slightly larger and again gave the impression of perhaps being greenish rather than the usual red of Marta's desert surface. However, as Canove had moved on from the observation team and the workload had increased, she simply filed the new image, noted the observation, and moved on. This happened again for the next three years before Jai herself was moved to a new position and a junior surveyor took her place. He noticed that his predecessor had humorously labelled the dark patch 'Black Forest', but since other features on the planet had been given fanciful names, he thought no more about it.

Some twenty- five years later, new interest was triggered in the survey group when a file of ancient planetary images became available from before the Great Forgetting.* They had been restored from a few pre-

---

* A period in history, from around 2,020 to 2,600, when a series of global viral pandemics and resource wars reduced Earth's human population to less than thirty per cent, followed closely by a series of

served pages in ancient books discovered beneath the rubble of a ruined building on the island of Ingland. Ceral Postos was charged with comparing these old images with the most recent equivalents.

That's funny, thought Ceral. All the planetary surfaces look the same except for Marta. Much of Marta's surface seems to have changed from red to brownish green, and the change has spread out from a very small area first seen about thirty years ago. She knew that recent research meant it might be possible to obtain light spectra from the planet's surface; difficult in view of the distance to Marta but perhaps not impossible. She prepared a spectral request, including a set of images over time of the mysterious area on Marta's surface, and sent it to Spectral Research.

To her surprise, no less a person than the group's leader contacted her by FarSpeaker. He asked her to come and meet with the group the next day. Excitedly, he told her, 'This is a momentous discovery. We want you be present as one of the researchers when we announce it.'

The next day, when Ceral arrived at Spectral Research headquarters, she was surprised to be met by the leader and taken into a meeting of the group as an honoured guest. She was introduced as the person who had made the most significant discovery in modern history. What on Earta have I done, she thought. I only asked for a spectral analysis. She soon understood. The leader invited a young researcher to present his findings for the dark area on Marta's surface that had come to be known as 'Black Forest'.

'These,' he concluded, 'are the absorption and fluorescence spectra of chlorophyll. Black Forest is indeed a patch of plant life, closely related biochemically to plant life on Earta. 'But further, there are also signs of an iron-haeme compound – not haemoglobin but something similar, possibly with affinity to compounds found in some bacteria on Earta.'

------

violent solar storms whose radiation destroyed all computer chips and digitally stored records at the time. Both existing knowledge and education systems were comprehensively destroyed, with the consequence that much had to be rediscovered. This process continues.

This momentous discovery led to the Universal Life (UniLife) Theory, that all life in the universe has a common origin regardless of its form. It also led to the biggest controversy since the Great Forgetting, one side believing that life had pre-existed in scattered sites throughout the universe since creation by a higher being, and the other believing that life on Marta was seeded from Earta; that it came from the legendary ill-fated first manned Marta probe, presumed to have crashed on Marta when solar storms destroyed its guidance systems. According to the legend, two astronauts and hydroponic algal cultures were on the flight. The astronauts would have died on impact, but their anaerobic bacterial symbionts and some cultured blue-green algal cells just might have survived.

The controversy continues.

Defending the family

I hear a rustling in the leaves, and the faint scratching of claws on the bark of our tree. I take my head out from under my wing and look towards the nest. It is still dark but first light is showing in the east. Wookita still has her head under her wing and has not heard the noise. The soft stirrings of our little ones are a feather-light murmur below her in the nest. From across the paddock, the neighbour magpies' morning carolling rings out, waking Wookita.

Now, in the faint light of dawn, I can see a dark shadow against the trunk of the tree a little below the nest. I call with alarm, 'Danger! Cat!'

Answering alarm calls echo from several nearby trees. Everyone knows the call for danger in all our languages. The menacing shadow freezes against the tree trunk trying for invisibility. I am not fooled. I call 'Danger' again as loudly as I can, hoping to convince the predator that he is discovered and might as well give up. The rustlings and calls of disturbed neighbour birds are all around us now.

The cat must be feral and hungry – the most dangerous sort. He knows he is discovered but still moves a couple of claw-holds up the trunk towards the nest. If I were not protecting the nest, I would fly off and away. No sense in tempting a cat unnecessarily. But now, at this time of year, I must protect Wookita and the little ones. The need to protect is stronger than the need to escape. I hop to a closer branch and call danger again, as loudly as I can.

The pointed things on top of a cat's head are a good place to strike, so I take off and strike one as hard as I can with my beak, landing afterwards on another branch close by. The cat gives a yowl of pain and turns to look at where the attack came from. I can see two yellow eyes. Without thinking of the danger, I take off towards one of the eyes, strike it with my beak as hard as I can, and fly on through to another branch. The cat yowls loudly and lets go of the bark with its front claws, flailing to find and strike me. I cannot let fear make me freeze. I have to continue attacking until the cat is gone.

Wookita joins me on a nearby branch and screeches another danger call. Now we both attack, one each side of the cat's head. I drive my beak into the other yellow eye. This time, the cat lets go altogether and we hear it swishing and thumping through the branches towards the ground. When it lands, some of our neighbour birds form a mob around it, screeching and pecking.

Finally, the cat gives up and runs away across the paddock, still followed by an attacking mob. We have done it. The danger is gone for now.

Back on the home branch, Wookita is hushing the little ones. They have their heads up over the rim of the nest and are chittering with alarm. We hope their first exciting adventure has taught them a vital lesson about cats!

Reflections on frogs

Response to a challenge to write on a single topic in 50 words, 100 words and 200 words

If you stand beside our local pond and listen, you can hear three layers of frog song: 'creakers' make a high-pitched creaking, 'croakers' sing similarly but deeper in tone. Bonkers make deep 'bonk' calls. If they crawl into a pipe, the bonk sounds like a loud trombone note!

*

Why are French people called 'frogs'? Possibly it's because they eat frogs' legs. But they have other interesting quirks too.

I shared an office for several months with a French scientist. He loved mature Camembert cheese and fine French cognac, delicacies which needed sophisticated shopping to source. In the interests of improving international relationships, he shared these liberally with the research team, giving several of us mild addictions to both!

He also had a taste for the prettiest, long-legged, blonde female students on campus. To progress these relationships, he combined cognac with sweet treats from a local patisserie. Enough said!

*

Remember when the French secret services bombed the Greenpeace ship *Rainbow Warrior* in Auckland harbour, killing a crew member? The French were testing nuclear weapons in the Pacific, and the ship was preparing for a protest voyage into the testing zone. Having recently come from New Zealand to join a research team at Melbourne University, I was outraged by this French act of war – furious in fact!

When the university asked me to host a visit from the French minister for science to explain my research, I told them I would not be able to stay civil. They must have thought I was joking, however, as they kept me in the program.

What an opportunity for personal protest! I went and bought a magnificent, large, toy frog. He was made of green felt with yellow spots and long floppy legs. He looked even more fetching with a rope around his neck tied in a proper hangman's noose. I hung him in the doorway of my laboratory accompanied by a big placard saying, *Jouez avec votre bomb chez vous!** and then departed home for the day.

My protest actually became a local funny story for quite some time.

.

* Play with your bomb in your own backyard!

Weep for the river: the limits of trust

The Savannah River flows down from the Appalachian range, slowing gradually as it crosses the Piedmont to the port of Savannah, and finally meandering through coastal swamps to the sea. Some sections of the journey resemble the blackwater reaches of the Florida Everglades, with stands of swamp cypresses in seemingly motionless water surrounded by their woody 'knees', and occasional thickets of cattails with the green scum of duckweed caught around their stems. Here and there, on a branch above the water, an anhinga sits, back to the warmth of the sun, drying its wings. The quiet of the humid air is broken only by the whir of dragonflies and the occasional splash of a water creature breaking the surface of its pool. In its natural state, this land is serene and beautiful.

In the middle reaches of the river's journey between Georgia and South Carolina, sit a nuclear power station on the Georgia side and, on the South Carolina side, the 'Savannah River Site'. This latter site is a huge two-hundred-thousand-acre swath of access-controlled military land, one of the most contaminated nuclear sites in the world. While its presence is public knowledge, little information beyond comforting spin is readily available.

This was the site of America's nuclear bomb-making program in the Cold War era – five nuclear reactors arranged on the land in a pattern to defeat any single straight-line bombing run. They were commissioned to manufacture tritium and plutonium and, while decommissioned now, have left a deadly legacy on the site. There have, of course, been accidental deaths from radiation, and many cases of cancer, particularly in the early gung-ho days of the facility, and particularly among the black workers on the site.

For much of the Cold War, America and the Soviet Union pursued a strategy of Mutually Assured Destruction – MAD by name and MAD by nature. For America, this involved keeping loaded B52 nuclear bombers in the air at all times, serviced by aerial fuel tankers. Just how MAD this scheme actually was became obvious in 1966 when a refuelling operation over Spain went horribly wrong. A tanker plane crashed, together with the laden bomber it was servicing. Three hydrogen bombs landed in an Andalusian farming village and one fell just offshore in the Mediterranean. As the bombs were not armed, a monstrous deadly explosion was avoided, but there was extensive contamination of agricultural land by radioactive plutonium. Fifteen hundred tons of contaminated soil were shipped back to the States in steel drums and buried on the Savannah River site.

Most of the Savannah River Site may need to be off-limits to humans for some hundreds of thousands of years. The scale of the contamination is mind-blowing! The half-life of plutonium, the time it will take for half of what's there to be gone, is twenty-four thousand years. For all the plutonium on the site to become harmless could take around two hundred and forty thousand years, longer than modern humans have walked the earth. The manufacture of such a deadly legacy is indeed MAD.

Today, the site is home to a research institute, euphemistically described as investigating radionuclides and nuclear clean-up technologies. There is also a large concrete pond like a giant swimming pool for underwater storage of spent nuclear fuel rods from the original reactors, the nuclear power stations across the river in Georgia, and many other interstate nuclear power facilities. This spent fuel no longer generates power, but it is by no means benign. To keep the rods cool, water is pumped from the river, circulated through the pool and pumped back into the river via a tributary creek. The hot water is yet another form of contamination. If you look across from the Georgia power station, you can see the creek and adjacent stretches of river are edged with dying swamp cypresses, unable to handle the raised temperature of the water or leaking radioactivity.

Elsewhere on the site, waste that has leached into the ground water over time is allowed to accumulate in a dam, said to be inhabited by two large alligators that have been named 'Tritigator' and 'Plutogator' for the toxic waste in the water.

A substantial number of deer also live inside the secure boundary fences of both this site and the power station across the river. In the absence of predators, their numbers increase over time. Every few years, the local amateur deer hunters are invited in with their guns to perform a cull. They are carefully assigned to defined areas and hunt with staff minders. At the end of the day, they are feted with a big spit-roast pork barbecue, but the deer carcasses are taken away and buried. They are too contaminated to eat!

I visited the area of the Georgia power station and the Savannah River Site in the 1980s. It left a deep impression on me. What a frightening piece of work is the human animal! Could we ever trust the controllers of an industrial-military state?

A great legacy

The first I knew of any legacy was when a delivery driver came to the door with a battered box wrapped in brown paper. I verified that it was indeed addressed to me and then signed for the delivery. I wrestled the box in the door and set it down in the living room. I didn't recognise the sender's name, but the address – Shell Cottage, St Ives, Cornwall, UK –, rang a distant bell.

Full of curiosity, I began unwrapping. Underneath the paper was a plain cardboard box. I slit the tape holding it closed, and lifted the flaps to find an envelope with my name on it. The letter inside was written on onionskin paper in spidery handwriting.

Dearest Elizabeth,

I wonder if you can remember me. We met years ago when your parents came to visit St Ives. You would have been only about four years old, such a sunny little thing. How you adored the sea, the shells and the rock pools. I would have loved for you to stay longer but your parents had other places to visit, so we only had a few weeks to get to know each other. Somehow, time has slipped away so now even the memories are almost gone.

I have learned that I don't have much time left. Don't be sad. I'm not. I've had a long and wonderful life. Years ago, when you visited, I had just taken over the family home and business. Perhaps you might still have a few memories of an old shop full of crafts, souvenirs, and art supplies; and even perhaps of the little cottage through the door in the back wall. The shop did very well for me, bringing me a good living and many friends and interesting conversations.

When my brother Eddie, your grandfather, migrated to Tasmania years ago, we lost touch. He had fallen out with Father and, in any event, neither of us were much for writing. He was too interested in a mining career, while I was only interested in painting. I never did marry, but both Eddie and our other brother Sam married and had sons.

More recently, as the shop became too much for me, your cousin Tamsin, Sam's granddaughter, helped by coming to work with me. A few hours a week at the start gradually grew to full-time, with me only dropping in for chats and pottering about.

I don't have much to leave in my will, and not many people to leave it to. You and Tamsin are my only surviving relatives. I trust you will understand why I am leaving her the shop as she depends on it for her living. While the contents of this box may not seem like much of a legacy, I trust you will take the time to read and look at it all. It represents all the things we might have talked about if you had grown up in St Ives. I hope it can give you at least some inkling of our family's lives and times.

When you receive this box, I will be gone. Please don't grieve for me. Be joyful that you can share the things inside. And one day, if you have the chance, call in to visit Shell Cottage. The mementos in this box will give you much to talk about with Tamsin.

With all my affection and best wishes,

Your Great Auntie Mattie

I put the letter down almost without thinking. My inner eyes were fixed on a distant memory of a little cottage shop, the treasures that filled it, and the warm, friendly lady who lived behind it. I made a deal with myself to unpack the box slowly and look at everything properly in sequence. Somehow it seemed the respectful thing to do.

That humble box proved a treasure trove. Inside were family diaries, letters, and photographs dating back to the time of Auntie Mattie's own grandparents. Every night after work, I lost myself in learning how the saga of British history affected one family in one corner of the old Empire.

I experienced the change from horses to automobiles, then trains and planes. I saw the changing fashions, and the changes to working lives. I heard about the Empire, the hardships suffered by the rural poor, and the impact of two world wars. I saw the decline in fishing and the rise of tourism. I met many relatives I had barely, or never, heard about. I read of their births, marriages and deaths, their joys and sorrows, all from a family point of view.

Now I can feel my family roots even while living half a world removed. I can't wait to visit St Ives again. Thank you, Auntie Mattie. What a great legacy!

Inspiration

Response to a challenge to write a story in 150 words or less

Standing by the open grave in the earth floor, where a woman weeps over her dead child, the shaman murmurs a spell to keep the child's spirit in the home forever, as the father gently lays the hearth stone back into place.

In today's world, an aspiring writer lifts a heavy stone in an overgrown garden and takes the mysterious bones beneath for archaeological study. He is told the bones are those of a young boy who died three thousand years ago.

In a dream, the dead child pleads with the writer to take him home, so after the analysis he brings the bones home, placing the little skull on a shelf in his study.

From this day on, vivid dreams allow him to write such convincing 'fiction' about prehistoric village life that he becomes a celebrated author.

The blank page

Nervously, I opened the envelope and drew out a single folded sheet of blank paper. The sender's name had triggered a dread I thought conquered years ago. I laid the seemingly innocent white page on the desk and looked it over carefully – both sides. I held it up to the light. There was no clue to its contents; no faint markings; nothing resembling a microdot or other crypto device. I took out a magnifying glass and looked again; still nothing. The blank page just lay on the desk, mute, blind and mysterious. I left it there and went away to think while doing other things.

A couple of days later, the paper was still just as mysterious. It had been sent by Phillipe Legrand, but the address was unfamiliar. Phillipe and I had parted in unhappy circumstances many years ago, and I had not heard from him since. I saw him again in my mind's eye: tall, dark and frowning, with the slight stoop of someone who spent his life poring over books.

Years ago, when I was a young student studying the preservation of ancient documents, Phillipe gave me my first part-time job in the private back room of his antiquarian bookshop. The work, with its quiet, almost tomb-like environment and accompanying smell of dusty old manuscripts, was magic to me. I learned so much from him about many aspects of old books, and enjoyed my brief, cheerful chats with his wife Jeanette during tea breaks.

Then it all fell apart. A valuable book went missing – one I had been working on just the previous day, worth many thousands of dollars. I knew I had left it open on the table to work on further the next day, but how could I prove it? Phillipe called the police, who came with forensic equipment to examine the work room, and the tapes from the in-store CCTV. They found my fingerprints on the worktable and adjacent books of course, and those of Phillipe, but that was all. If the book had been stolen, the thief must have worn gloves and somehow avoided the cameras going in and out of the back room.

Time dragged on. The police investigation went nowhere and eventually the case was set aside with no conclusion. The bookshop atmosphere had become toxic, and even my friendly chats with Jeanette had come to an end. Phillipe remained suspicious and eventually fired me from my job. To be honest, by that stage it was almost a relief. I found a new job in the university library and tried to forget about Phillipe's bookshop. I hadn't heard from him since I left, many years ago, so why was he contacting me now?

Over time, curiosity got the better of me. Why had Phillipe sent me a blank sheet of paper? I mailed a query to him at the unfamiliar address. A few days later, a reply came back from what sounded like a retirement home or hospital, giving me a phone number and asking me to contact the office.

When I called, a pleasant-sounding woman answered the phone. I gave my name and she said, 'Oh, I'm so sorry, Ms Marchant. Mr Legrand passed away recently. We found a letter and a wrapped parcel in his wardrobe addressed to you. There were also instructions for us to send the letter and, once you contacted us, to ask you to come and collect the parcel. Obviously, he can't give it to you himself now. Would you like us to mail it to you?'

Of course I agreed. Then spent the next several days speculating about what the parcel contained.

When it arrived, it was heavily wrapped in padded packing and strong parcel tape. I unwrapped it carefully. Inside the padded layers were a large, old book and another letter. The book looked like the one that had gone missing years ago. How could that be?

Phillipe's letter explained.

Dear Sophie,
	Please accept this book with my very humble apologies for the

injustice I did you years ago. I should have known you didn't steal it. I should have trusted you.

Because it was a reported valuable antique, the police returned it recently when it turned up in a proceeds-of-crime confiscation. The book has a current value of at least twenty thousand dollars. As recompense for the injustice, I leave it to you to decide whether to keep or sell it. Either way, I hope it now brings you good luck.

I had hoped to see you again and apologise in person, but there is little time left. If you are reading this letter, then time has run out.

I'm so sorry, Sophie. Please forgive me for my stupidity.

Respectfully and, yes, affectionately

Phillipe

Mary's change crusade

Mary was adamant that something needed to change. Her school course on sustainable living, together with media coverage of worldwide school strikes for climate action, had raised her awareness to heights that bemused her parents. It was like a sudden religious conversion.

'Mum, Dad, we have to live more sustainably, with less water, less electricity and less fossil fuel. We need to stop being consumers and start being conservers. We need to eat less meat, make less waste and stop using plastics. It's really urgent if the world is going to survive.'

She took a deep breath and continued. 'You know, the economy isn't actually about money. It's really just a giant machine for turning resources into garbage. When the government promotes economic growth, they're just trying to make us run the garbage machine faster and faster. Pretty soon, the resources will be gone, and we'll have so much garbage in the oceans and atmosphere our quality of life will be trashed. Can't you see? It's already started, and kids like us will have to deal with it. How can we sit and do nothing?'

Mary's mum and dad sat back in their chairs, astounded at this level of passion coming from a teenager. They too were concerned by global warming, but felt the problem was too huge for one family to have any impact.

Mary's brother Richie was no help either. His level of concern was at the opposite end of the spectrum from Mary's. 'I don't use resources,' he declared. 'I just use my phone and iPad. I'm happy to eat vegetarian fries with every meal, and wear my jeans and T-shirts until they fall off me. If you all just leave me alone, I'm quite happy to have only one shower a week and spend most of my time in my room.'

'Pooh!' said Mary. 'You could single-handedly pollute our whole home environment like that!'

'Well,' said Mary's dad. 'I think Mary's correct. As just one family in the whole world, we can't do much, but if every family did what they could, things would start to change. Mary, how about you use your school notes to set up a sustainable living plan for us.'

So that's what Mary did. She put into it everything she had learned in the sustainable living course. It was a great plan, comprehensive, thoughtful – and about ten pages long!

When she presented it to the family after dinner one evening – reading the whole document in the process – the others greeted it in stunned silence.

'You're mad,' said Richie, getting up and leaving the room.

Mum and Dad were more diplomatic.

'Mary,' said Mum, 'we just can't do all that. It means a complete change in how we live our lives. It means lots of expensive renovations to the house, a new car, and things we just can't afford to deal with at the moment.'

'Don't get us wrong,' said Dad, 'it's a great plan, and if everyone did all those things I'm sure we could save the earth. The trouble is we can't do everything all at once. What you've listed will take at least ten years or more. We need to start with small things we can do easily, and then move on to the bigger things.'

Mary was crestfallen. She was so keen to move to a better future right away.

'Tell you what,' said Mum, 'why don't you go back and reorganise the plan. Change the headings from Electricity, Water, Transport, Food, and so on. It will be easier to follow if you reorganise it under different headings like Things to do today, Things to do next month, Things to do next year, and so on, finishing up with Things to save up for.'

Mary brightened up again. It seemed changes might be possible after all. 'OK,' she said. 'I'll go and do it.'

So that's how Mary's family began their sustainability journey the very next day, by creative use of dinner leftovers in another meal, switching off everything not in use, piggybacking several errands into one car trip, taking shorter showers and flushing the toilet less.

Even Richie could cope with that!

Atonement

Response to a challenge to write a story in 200 words or less

Nick felled the terrified elderly woman with one blow. She lay, groaning, as he searched the bedroom. Finding a jewellery box and some cash, he tossed them into his backpack and ran, crunching across glass from the broken window.

The cash soon went on drugs, but something held him back from fencing the jewellery. He couldn't forget her look of terror and groans of pain. Long-buried feelings surfaced as an inner voice saying, 'How would you feel if it happened to your gran?'

Nick considered his ruined life and decided to get help. After months in rehab, he was confident enough to return to normal living. The first thing he did was find the elderly woman.

She had recovered slowly. It wasn't just the broken arm; it was also the fear that kept her awake at night. Nick knocked on her door and gave her back the jewellery box with extra cash inside. He asked to be forgiven and explained how he had changed. He also offered to run errands for her when she needed help.

In time, they developed an unlikely friendship – and both slept much better at night!

View from the old windmill

From the old shepherd's hut, you can see right across the valley to the distant Boorumu Hills. Early in the morning, if the light's right, they look as though someone covered them with a blanket, the soft blue, brown and green folds flowing down to the valley floor, down to the line of gums along the upside-down river meandering along the far side of the plain.

Our old shepherd, Lennie, who use to live out here, told me years ago about the upside-down river. Water from the hills is down there, deep in the sand, flowing slowly along the line of gums. He showed me how to find it, by choosing a patch of deep shade under one of the gums, digging down and waiting for the bottom of the hole to fill with brown, gritty water. He said it's the same water that's pumped up by the windmill here in front of the shepherd's hut, but it takes hundreds of years to filter across underneath the plain. Once, years ago, he told me, there was so much rain the upside-down river turned right way up, with water flowing along the surface and spreading out onto the plain. They used to run a big mob of sheep out here in those days. But I haven't seen any water flowing like that in my lifetime. Now it's only a rest camp on the southern drove line.

Lennie doesn't come out here any more; he says he's too old to spend two whole days on a horse. Now, when we need to drive a mob through the valley to the road for market, I come down the day before to get the mill going, pump water to the tank, fill the trough, mend the stock-yard fence, and clean out the hut. If there are any rats or other little critters around, Razza, my dog, has a great time rousting them. He never actually catches anything but he has fun trying. I always keep a close eye on him to make sure he's not rousting a snake.

I came down yesterday and got it all set up for the mob to come through by tonight. It took a while, as the gears of the windmill had rusted up a lot since last time and needed some hard levering and a lot of oil to get moving. But there's a good sound to listen to now. Instead of just the flapping of a loose sheet of iron on the wall of the hut when the wind gets up, there's the steady creak of the windmill and the sound of water trickling into the tank.

There's nothing Razza and I can do now except sit in the shade under the tank till the heat goes out of the sun. Then I'll pull a few bales of hay out of the stack in the back of the hut and throw them over the fence into the yard – just enough for the sheep to snack on tonight before they move on in the morning.

I can see the dusty spirals of a couple of willy-willies far out in the middle of the plain. I hope they stay out there and don't come this way. Once, I had one come across this side and over the hut; but that once was bad enough. I was chewing grit for hours and shaking it out of my hair and clothes for days. Razza just curled up behind the tank with his tail over his nose and whined. Afterwards, he was shaking himself and scratching for quite a while. I guess willy-willies are just what happens in a long drought like we have now, when there's been no rain for years and the plants have begun to die and blow away leaving only red dust behind.

Maybe Razza and I dozed off a bit. Now, shadows are starting to mark out the valleys and ridges of the hills, and the sun is sliding down the sky. I stand, stretch and look up the valley to the north, squinting a bit with freshly woken-up eyes. Yes, I can just make out the first signs – the dust raised by many little feet now rising above the plain like distant smoke. The mob is on its way.

Round the bend

My life went round a corner that year; well, actually, you could say it went right round the bend!

I was working as a contract bench scientist in Melbourne, when the project leader called me into his office and dropped a bombshell:

'I'm afraid this year's news from the ARC* isn't good. While we've had three-year grants ever since the project started, this year, they feel the science is almost complete and one more year should see it go out to industry. I'm sorry but I can only offer you your job for one more year.'

Well, that was a blow. Ever since high school, I had planned a career as a scientist. Back then, it was a prestigious choice – not quite up to the standard of doctor or lawyer, but not that far behind. It's difficult, however, to plan a career on a year-by-year basis, especially with qualifications like mine in an obscure science field. Long-term jobs in plant cell biology were as rare as hens' teeth. I didn't want to cause a questionable break in my science career, so I immediately started scanning professional job advertisements.

With six months of my contract left, I was desperate. Australia had absolutely nothing suitable on offer, so I started looking at international openings. After some weeks, I finally found one – at the University of Kentucky, Lexington, in the USA. From the description, the job could have been made especially for me. It involved an initial five-year contract with potential for eventual permanent employment. Unfortunately, Lexington is essentially the antipodes of Melbourne. It was about as far away as I could go! I mulled it over for a few days. It would be a huge leap of faith to take on such a move. But beggars can't afford to

* Australian Research Council

be choosers, and neither could I. Deciding to at least try my luck, I mailed off an application letter and my freshly polished CV.

Imagine my huge surprise when I received a letter back asking me to come for an interview at university expense. Was this for real – I mean, who goes right around the world for a plant cell biology interview? Do they actually know where Australia is? This outfit must be rolling in funds to bring interviewees from the other side of the earth! Maybe they think I live in Melbourne, Florida!

With a rather nervous mental leap into the unknown, I gathered up my research results into what I hoped would be an acceptable interview seminar, and embarked on the long journey: Melbourne to Auckland, Auckland to Los Angeles, Los Angeles to Cincinnati, and Cincinnati to Lexington. Believe me, I was bushed by the time I arrived!

I was met by a delightful young staff member from the university's School of Agriculture, who drove me to a hotel. He gave me a printed program for the next three days, including tours of various parts of the campus, visits with relevant staff, and the all-important seminar to staff and students followed by a social and final interview with the dean. After organising my pick-up for the morning, he left me to get on with some serious rest; and, I have to say, that hotel bed felt divine.

The next three days were a blur. The agriculture staff and students were interested and respectful. The research facilities were excellent. The only sour note came from observing that the janitorial staff were all black and sat on the floor in the corridor for their coffee break because no other facility was provided for black staff! The departmental secretaries were dressed like southern belles with frilly floral dresses and ribbons in the back of their long hair. My outfit of tight jeans, knee-high boots and tooled leather belt and hat must have looked to them like something out of *Crocodile Dundee*!

Finally, the all-important research seminar. The lecture room was crowded for such a novelty speaker. All went well until I referred to pollen-style self-incompatibility as 'the premature ejaculation syndrome of the plant world' (which it is, in fact, as it involves ejection of sperms too early to get to the egg). After a mass gasp and a few seconds of stunned silence, there was a mighty roar of laughter. The whole room relaxed and questioning after the presentation and the following social was free and easy.

Later, in my final visit to the dean's office before the long journey back to Melbourne, I was told the job was mine if I wanted it.

So that's how I ended up spending six years as a 'resident alien' in the deep south of the USA – through the unintended consequence of career desperation!

Here's to good-hair days!

Dear Sandie,

I'm sorry it has been such a long time since I last wrote. When I looked at my calendar this morning, I was shocked to find it has been over two years. Please forgive me.

Your last letter arrived around a year ago but, unfortunately, it hit me at a time when I was not capable of talking or writing to anyone. After such good news about your throat cancer cure, I should have sent a joyful letter back to you. The fact that I didn't was a terrible way to treat my oldest school friend. And the longer I delayed, the harder writing seemed to get. Well, here's to putting that right!

The way you tackled your battle with cancer was so inspirational. In spite of the horror of cancer and the sickness caused by chemo, your letters were filled with the things you were doing, and the ones you were going to do some day. I don't know how you managed to stay so upbeat. Do you remember sending me that picture of you in a bright green 'fright' wig? I couldn't help laughing aloud at the fly-away hair and sexy pout. Yes, it was a laugh, but it made a deep impression on me. It spoke of incredible courage, acceptance of whatever life brings, and a determination not to succumb without a damn good fight!

I know you still have to wait a few years for a final all-clear but, at this point, it is looking like a clean cure. I have my fingers crossed for you. I hope you are getting to do a lot of those activities you were planning during your chemo.

At the time your last letter arrived, I had just, the week before, received my own diagnosis of bowel cancer. I was terrified. I wanted to run and hide from the whole world. I couldn't bear to talk or write to anyone. It was as though I had just frozen up inside. I even considered finding some way to end it all, and might well have done so if the means had been easily available.

I had an urgent operation to remove the tumour, followed immediately by starting chemo. I was weak, depressed and as sick as a dog with every round. How you kept your courage up while you were on chemo I'll never know!

When I remembered your inspirational courage, though, it made a huge difference. I decided that, whatever it cost, I was going to climb out of the hole. As my hair fell out in handfuls, I got hold of a big purple fright wig. The enclosed photo is my answer to your green wig. I realise now that the in-your-face wig was a part of your clever answer to depression and sickness. Who can wallow in misery when everyone around them is actually laughing and smiling in sympathy rather than being all dismal!

I know now that you were telling me, 'Well, if I have to lose my hair for a while, why not make the most of it? Why try to hide the problem under a scarf or beanie. Put it out there and let everyone enjoy it!'

So that's what I've been doing, and I now appreciate your clever secret strategy. When I see the people around me stare and smile at my outrageous wig, I feel better somehow – as though I am not just a vision of sickness but also a source of cheerfulness and fun.

I don't know what the eventual outcome will be. It appears the surgery and chemo have defeated the cancerous beast for now but, of course, it will be a few years before anyone knows for sure.

For the last few rounds of chemo, my treatment has been changed to a milder drug that doesn't make me feel so sick, and my hair is just starting to grow back again into a silky urchin cut. Soon I will be giving up the purple wig – but, you know what, I am actually going to miss it!

Well, that's it from me for now. I promise not to delay so long with the next letter. Next time, I hope I will have other news that doesn't come from the sickroom.

Thank you seems like such a small word for all you have done, even at such a distance, to give me courage through a very dark time – but, small word or not, thank you, Sandie, from the bottom of my heart.

May your life be filled with one good hair day after another. Happy Birthday Girl!

Love from Margie

Distancing grief

Copenhagen, turn of the twentieth century

The funeral was over, the mourners gone, and the family departed to their rooms with final tears and comforting hugs. Finally giving in to his own private grief, George sat down in his chair by the fire, dropped his face into his hands and allowed the long-denied tears to slide through his fingers.

'Oh, my love, how could you leave me? Our children are grown. We could have shared long happy years together if you had stayed yet a while. How can I live without you? How can I stay in this home we built together and filled with our love? It is too empty, too cold, and the god you prayed to every night is now just an empty vessel filled with false promises. Forgive me. I just cannot bear it.'

He couldn't face returning alone to the bed he had shared for so many years with his beloved wife. Not this night, nor the next, nor the many nights after that. The Black Dog that came to torment him every winter, now much fiercer since his wife's death, had him firmly in its grip. He slept fitfully on the settle beside the fireplace, frequently experiencing tortured dreams and waking to tears.

His five young adult children, Jan, Marika, Christian, Pieter and Johan, became seriously worried about him. They continued to run the small family farm on the outskirts of Copenhagen in the way they had learned since they were young. Their father, however, seemed unable to lift himself back into any form of participation. He spent long hours sitting by the door overlooking the neat kitchen garden that his wife had planted so lovingly the previous spring. Sometimes he seemed to be talking to her under his breath. Every Sunday, he went to church with the family as usual, but now he no longer entered the church with them. Even on cold and snowy days, he sat forlornly, bundled in a coat and rug, beside her grave or in the porch until the service was over and they came to find him.

Gradually, the weather warmed, the snow melted, and spring dressed the land in fresh green. Slowly the Black Dog retreated, allowing George to remember his wife without weeping. He remembered how she wanted her children to travel and see lands far away before they settled down with families.

'I hear you, my love,' he murmured to himself late one night as the fire burned to embers beside him. 'I'll talk with the family about it tomorrow.'

The following evening, when the family gathered for supper, he raised the topic of selling the farm and moving to a new land where winters were not so cold and dark. He told them how their mother had wanted them to travel, and how he felt, right to the bottom of his heart, that he could not stay on the farm without her.

His children surprised him. He thought they would be reluctant to leave the place where they were born, but they were excited and eager to explore possibilities. They understood his need to leave the home he had shared with their mother. For many nights, they discussed ideas, ranging across all types of occupations in lands such as Canada, America, South America and Australia.

Jan, who wanted to become a Lutheran minister, thought there would be good opportunities in America, Canada or Australia. Marika, who wanted to write and paint, thought that any of those lands would be good. Christian and Pieter wanted to take advantage of the growing fashion for exercise therapy and found a school of physical culture. The two wealthy Australian cities of Sydney and Melbourne seemed like the best prospects. Johan wasn't sure what he wanted to do, but was happy to join Christian and Pieter in their business and then look at other opportunities once they had established themselves in a new land.

Their father had a strong desire to go as far away from his wife's grave as possible. He knew that, while beautiful memories of their love would travel with him, much of the sadness would stay at her graveside. For him, the best place seemed to be the emerging settlement of Hobart Town in Van Diemen's Land, half a world away on the southern side of Australia.

After much discussion, that was what the family decided to do. After selling the farm and animals for a good price, they booked passage on a ship travelling to Australia. They disembarked at Hobart Town while the ship went on in ballast to load a cargo of wheat in Melbourne.

Now, over a century later, their family name still echoes down through Australia's history, associated with state politics, a novel that was made into an early Australian film, oil paintings of Tasmanian landscapes, and a school of physical culture which has survived to the present.

Running from his grief turned out, in the end, to be the best gift George could have given both his family and his adopted country.

Bushfire

Farmer Pete Barrie cursed as his tractor bounced over deep corrugations in the dirt road, shaking the reading glasses out of his shirt pocket. He stopped the tractor and got down to retrieve them but found the lenses broken. With another eloquent curse, he kicked what was left onto the road verge, climbed back onto the tractor and drove away. It would be easy enough to get another pair when he drove past the pharmacy in Harrietville.

He had no idea of the wider impact of this minor, irritating incident.

The consequences began later with a small shard of broken lens shining dazzlingly in the hot afternoon sun. From the tinder-dry grass below rose a thin wisp of smoke, drifting lazily in the shimmering air. On a dead leaf, a small black spot grew and became a hole. For a few seconds, the hole grew larger as its rim curled and charred. Then the leaf burst into flame and fell into the litter as an ember. It was tiny, but it was enough. As it fell, it ignited other dry leaves and a little scrap of discarded paper. The wisp of smoke became a small fire, moving slowly across the verge into the adjacent dry scrub. Fed by leaf litter, dead twigs, and a strengthening northerly, it grew and spread, becoming a line of flame under a column of grey smoke.

Animals and birds downwind of the fire began to scent smoke – the smell of fear. A small mob of kangaroos came to their feet in the shade of the mallee gums, raised their heads to sniff the wind, then bounded away to the south. They were followed by birds, calling in alarm as they rose from the trees. An echidna waddled down into a shallow dip and dug himself deep into the shaded sand where a hint of moisture still lingered. A pair of hawks and a wedge-tailed eagle soared just ahead of the flames, waiting for small animals to run from the fire in panic, unaware of a second deadly threat above them.

The fire now had a voice – the crackle and snap of burning sticks. It climbed into the branches of tall shrubs and up the loose bark of trees. Flames began spiralling upwards twisting in their own hot updraught. Smoke became a roiling dark cloud blowing ahead of the fire in the rising wind. Then, as flames climbed progressively higher, the crowns of trees began to explode into fireballs. The fire moved faster, leaping through the tops of the trees at frightening speed. It roared with the terrifying new voice of a firestorm. Trees now burned from the top down rather than the bottom up as the fire front accelerated across the scrublands.

As the afternoon wore on, the line of fire moved steadily south, growing broader and stronger as bright swirls of embers danced ahead of the searing flames. Behind the fire, the blackened landscape smoked eerily. Then, as daylight faded to a smoky, purple sunset, the fire leapt into glowing visibility on the hills behind the little coastal town with its row of beachside fishing shacks and a few small farms.

The townsfolk knew the fire was approaching. They had seen the smoke and called for help from the Country Fire Service. The call was logged but the location was difficult. The remote little town was served by only one narrow road which other tongues of fire had already cut with burning vegetation and fallen trees.

The local fire warden sounded the siren to call the townsfolk down to the surf club for instructions. In the gathering dusk, he told them a call for help had been logged but, thanks to several other fires along the access road, they were likely to be on their own when the fire front arrived. With grim faces, they digested the news that each household now had to make an impossible choice between attempting to stay and defend their home in the fading light or go, leaving their property to the fire.

The size of the flames now approaching the town was terrifying. On seeing the threat, most of the townsfolk decided to go – but where? The one access road was blocked. Panic spread. Most raced away to quickly collect family and valuables from the shacks, then drive down the boat ramp onto the beach, or even into the water's edge if possible.

Soon, a number of cars were drawn up along the waterline, with more cars following down the ramp. Visibility was so poor in the smoke that there were several collisions, further adding to the general panic. Flames were now moving into the town. With a crackling roar, the first shack went up, followed quickly by several others. Gum trees among the shacks exploded like fireworks. People wading beyond their cars in the waves turned their faces away from the searing heat and ducked down into the restless black water that reflected the flames like an image of hell.

Parents pulled children from cars and held them, floating. A horse and rider galloped through the smoke and plunged into the sea, the horse snorting in terror with embers in its mane. The bawling of cattle was briefly heard over the roar of the fire, but quickly fell silent. Even if the animals had been freed, it was much too late.

Embers rained down hissing as they hit the water. Several of the menfolk used buckets of seawater to douse embers that threatened the cars. One ember, escaping notice, was sucked under the bonnet of a car, which promptly ignited. Three teenage boys and two sheep dogs erupted out into the water with terrified shouts and barks. More shacks exploded into flames. It seemed as though the whole world was on fire.

But fire blown by a following wind towards the sea eventually has nowhere to go. After nearly an hour of devastating the little township, it was essentially burned out. Everything flammable was gone, leaving only smouldering embers in fallen tree trunks.

As if in a dream, the townsfolk struggled out of the water and gathered on the beach in shocked, waterlogged groups. It was obvious there were no houses to return to, but the surf club appeared to be intact, thanks to its galvanised-iron construction and bare sandy surrounds. Slowly, as if sleepwalking, the townsfolk retrieved their cars and drove or walked to the building. Sharing whatever rugs and spare clothes they could find in their cars, they settled down on the floor to wait for day-light and for help to arrive.

Three of the townsfolk were lost that day, all residents who had lingered to save their animals or homes. There was speculation, of course, about how the fire had started back there on a roadside north of the town – a cigarette butt, perhaps? Pete Barrie, however, was never to realise the catastrophic result of kicking his broken reading glasses onto the roadside in the sun.

Temple of the sun

I scrambled up the last few metres to the crest of the hill, stood for a moment to catch my breath, then turned east and walked down the crest of the ridge towards the cape.* I could see a promising flat place to sit partway down the slope overlooking the gannet colony. I walked down carefully as the ridge was narrow with patches of uncertain footing among the tussocks of grass and loose stones.

Reaching the small flat area at the top of the cliff above the rookery, I stood and relaxed in the sun. Ahead of me, out to the east was the great blue expanse of Pacific Ocean, calm today with the sun winking like diamonds off the rippled surface. The coast stretched left and right, with the cape standing out ahead like the prow of a ship, its distinctive terminal rock stack rearing up like a shark's tooth from below the surface.

The noise of the gannet colony, the combined calls of thousands of birds, rose up from below me like the playing of a wild, ethereal piper. Birds wheeled, dipped, and soared. Out to the east of the cape, where the darker ruffles of schooling fish were visible on the sea, the birds plunged like white and gold arrows, disappearing almost without a splash into the sea, and then flying up from the water with fish that they carried back to their young in the colony.

It was all so beautiful, wild, and unspoilt that I felt my heart leap with a surge of ecstasy, a great lightness of being. The warmth and light filled me with a feeling of complete oneness with nature. Spontaneously, I stretched my arms up in homage to the sun, the source of it all.

In that moment, I understood the ancient Egyptian pharaoh Akhenaten who declared the golden disc of the sun to be the one true

* Te Kauwae-a-Māui: the fishhook of Maui (also known as Cape Kidnappers)

god. He lived well before people could cope with a monotheistic religion, but I knew in my heart that he was more enlightened than any other seer or prophet of his time. I thought of the famous wall carving showing him sitting with his family under a sun disc, whose rays like little hands reached down to him with blessings. My outstretched arms now received the same timeless blessings, and my consciousness seemed to expand beyond oneness with nature to include oneness with human history as well. What a joy. This was nature as a truly sacred place.

I sat down overlooking the cape and the gannets. After some time, the warmth of the sun and the hypnotic effect of the bird calls made me lean back into the grass and drift into a state of just being – a welcome change from any need to be doing. I half-closed my eyes so that rainbows shone through my lashes against a wonderful warm blue. Time passed.

Later, as I carefully picked my way back down to the beach, I took with me a great sense of peace and serenity. Perhaps others feel this way after visiting a Christian cathedral, an Islamic mosque, or a place sacred to their own religion, but I knew my peace and serenity came from Nature and its 'Temple of the Sun'.

The rain has come

When I woke up, it was to the usual, clear dawn, with the sun sitting on the horizon like a giant orange ball. While the weather forecast had hinted at storms building, there was no trace of them at present. I turned away from the window, accustomed to this type of disappointment.

I dressed in my dusty work clothes and walked down the veranda steps to the ute. It was already loaded with hay and wheat for our few remaining sheep, now clustered restlessly along the southern fence bleating for food. We were fortunate to have received some donated feed trucked up to us from the mallee farmers of the Wimmera. Our own last hay crop had run out six months ago, and standing grass more than six months before that. Now, the paddocks stood empty, with only red dust as far as the eye could see. If the emergency feed ran out, what then? It was too hard to think about. It was better to concentrate on just getting through each new day.

We had been hand feeding now for over two years. I could hardly remember the look and scent of grass-covered paddocks, the softness in the air around a well-filled dam, the song of cicadas in the trees. How long had it been since I had seen a landscape of plenty? Way, way too long.

We had sent more than two- thirds of our flock to market last year, keeping only sufficient healthy breeders to start a recovery when the drought broke – if it ever did. It was hard to maintain optimism, as we now had no income and were dependent on savings and the charity of other farmers in more fortunate regions.

The hot, dry days seemed to run into each other in endless succession. Occasional clouds on the horizon produced distant rumbles of thunder, but any moisture they carried passed by in the distance. Occasionally, we could see grey curtains of rain beneath these teasing clouds, but it was too hot and dry for moisture to reach the ground.

Even the line of gum trees in the home paddock had given up. Most of them were now just skeletons, their bare branches hosting only crows or the odd wandering hawks scouting for dead sheep. Even the sparse shade they once provided was gone

When I finished feeding out, I drove back to the house for coffee, and took it out to the veranda. As I sat there, it dawned on me that there was something different about the feel of the morning. The heat was building as usual but something about the air felt different, softer somehow. The smell of the sheep and dust seemed more intense; and hadn't I nearly dropped the milk container when I went to put it back in the fridge? It was unusually slippery with condensation. The humidity must be rising.

I looked at the sky. Was the overhead deep, hard blue just a little bit mistier than it had been yesterday? It was hard to tell, so I stopped thinking about it, climbed back into the ute and drove to the hay shed to load the afternoon feed. There was plenty to do around the sheds and, by the time I cleaned out the ute, made a couple of minor repairs to the tray and loaded the next lot of feed, it was midday.

When I came out again, I could see the weather was definitely changing. High, thin cirrus clouds and a cooler breeze from the east were taking the heat out of the day. In the machinery bay, the jobs board showed some wagers scribbled up by the station hands before they left for the day's fence inspection. I could see the odds were still running strongly against rain.

Over lunch, Janet and I talked about the chance of rain. Janet, who had been keeping an eye out the window, said she thought it just might happen this time. I was not so sure. We had been disappointed too many times by fickle clouds. We turned on the radio and listened to the regional forecast. It seemed there was heavy rain to the east of us, and the chance of rain in our district had risen to eighty percent. I had to admit it was sounding more hopeful.

Later, as I was finishing the afternoon feed out, the station hands rode in fast from the east, whooping and waving their hats in the air.

'The rain has come! The rain has come! Send her down, Huey!'

A few minutes later, it arrived – heavy, solid rain. I climbed out of the ute, tore off my hat and shirt, and faced up into the sweetest shower I could remember in years.

'Thank you, Lord – and please keep it coming!'

The idle business card

They sat abandoned on a side table among the empty glasses and crumb-laden plates, half a dozen business cards left at the at the end of an ABARE (Australian Bureau of Agricultural and Resource Economics) conference networking session. I casually picked them up and scanned them. Did they feature anyone whose card I might find useful? No. All but one featured consultants whose details I knew were readily available from the speakers list in the conference program.

The one stranger in the bunch gave little away: 'The GOYA Solution', written boldly in red across a cartoon drawing of an artist's palette and brush. Lower down, in small font, was the name Kevin Everidge and an email address. I knew Goya was an eighteenth-century Spanish painter, but what was his name doing on a business card at an ABARE conference? I put the card into my conference sack thinking I might indulge my curiosity sometime and find out. Back at the office, in my rush to attend to other tasks, I tossed it into an 'all-sorts' box in the bottom drawer, where it sat for months, idle and forgotten.

The following year, I again attended the annual ABARE conference and its usual first-night networking social. During the evening, Mitch McNeil, an agribusiness consultant I knew came up with a colleague in tow. 'I'd like to introduce you to Kevin Everidge. We often work as partners on farmer focus groups.'

Wait a minute – did he say Kevin Everidge?

I quickly leapt in. 'Pleased to meet you, Kevin. We haven't met before, but I think I have a memorable business card of yours in a drawer at work. Are you "The GOYA Solution"?'

He laughed, and still chuckling said, 'Yes. It's a bit of an attention getter, isn't it?'

'It certainly got mine,' I responded. 'How on earth did you choose that as a business name? I can't imagine a more tenuous connection than agribusiness and an eighteenth-century artist.'

'Well,' he said, still chuckling, 'do you know the real factor that stops most farmers from improving their returns?'

'Money,' I said, hazarding a guess. 'It's the one that gets talked about all the time.'

'No, that's what most folks think, but money's not actually the basic problem for most farmers, although more money would always be nice. The main difficulty is inertia, get-up-and-go, the initiative to change what they've been doing all their lives – or, in the case of family farms, for generations. Most farmers know how to work within the systems they're familiar with, but many have problems putting new knowledge to work because it's usually complex and means changing a lot of what they're used to doing. Critics over the fence don't help either.'

'Well, that's understandable,' I replied, 'but I don't think the problem is limited to farmers. I think we all have issues with get-up-and-go when we're used to doing something one way and then have to change to another. But where does Goya come into it?'

'He doesn't,' responded Kevin with a grin. 'He pulled a card out of his pocket. 'GOYA is an acronym. It stands for Get Off Your Arse! The artist's palette logo is only to help make it memorable.'

Now it was my turn to laugh. 'That's a great name-logo combination. I certainly won't forget it. But what do you actually do with farmers?'

'Well, basically,' said Kevin, 'we convince farmers of the need for specific changes, depending on circumstances, and then help them set out the necessary steps in practical order. We use focus groups of around five to ten farmers to help each other with questions and suggestions. That way we generate enough peer pressure to get everyone off their arses and started, and provide ongoing support through the tough bits of getting new systems working.'

Mitch chimed in at this point. 'Kevin's process works well. When our teams operate as partners, I present new science and the case for change, while Kevin provides the punch to get everyone off their arse and give it a go.'

'What a great idea,' I complimented them. 'Farmers certainly need support these days in the face of climate change and evolving trade conditions. Information and peer support must be incredibly important. Good luck for future focus groups.'

At that point, we all went back to social networking, but the seed was sown. I have never forgotten the GOYA concept, so appropriate in so many walks of life, including my own.

When I returned to my office, I burrowed in the all-sorts box in the bottom drawer and found Kevin's business card from the previous year. 'Right, you rinky-dinky little piece of card,' I thought, 'you've been idle long enough in that box! It's time to live up to your own slogan and help me out here.'

I sat it at the front of the card holder on my desk to remind me that, when change was needed, GOYA was the way to start!

It never fails.

Barney still has what it takes

Barney pulls his overcoat more closely around himself and hunches his shoulders against the cold. The sun has disappeared behind rain clouds, and an unseasonable wind tosses the overhanging tree branches. He picks his way carefully along a narrow riverside path, made slippery by water and fallen leaves. With his balance becoming a bit iffy these days, he's glad he's brought his walking stick. Getting old is a bummer!

He clutches his shopping bag more tightly with the other hand and picks up his pace as much as he can. It will be good to get home out of this weather; perhaps to a nice drop of something bracing to drink in his comfy chair.

A little way behind Barney, young Eric is slouching along the same path with his head down. A hooded rain jacket hides his face as he tries to look as inconspicuous as possible. After seeing Barney in the supermarket earlier, he figures that an old codger doing the shopping might actually have some cash on him rather than just the new-fangled plastic stuff for buying things. Gradually, he's gaining on Barney. He's planning to close the distance, then suddenly speed up, grab the old geezer, knock him off his feet and go through his pockets before he knows what's hit him. With a bit of luck, he'll be able to lift enough off him for a fix, with some over for a meal later.

Unfortunately for young Eric, he's picked on the wrong old geezer. Barney is a retired secondary teacher with years of experience in handling teenage tearaways. Barney has eyes in the back of his head. Generations of naughty schoolkids don't know it, but this phenomenon actually exists. The reflections in the edges of his strong glasses mean Barney can actually see what's going on behind him, and checking this novel view has become a habit over many years.

Barney sees young Eric gradually coming up behind him looking decidedly shifty. He guesses what might happen and readies himself by setting down his shopping bag just off the path and pretending to blow his nose. He puts his handkerchief back in his pocket and takes hold of his walking stick in both hands.

Just as young Eric pounces, he whirls around and thrusts his walking stick between Eric's legs. Eric, taken completely by surprise, trips and catapults head-first into the river. The strong current carries him back the way they had come, towards the township.

Barney smiles to himself realising that, despite being taken for an old codger, he is still one step ahead of naughty boys. He picks up his shopping bag and resumes his walk home.

Life is good!

Fertile imagination

What wonderful fertile imaginations children have. Remember listening to your kids playing? Their games are an endless stream of creative invention.

When my children were quite young – about eleven, six, five and four, Tegan the eldest used her vivid imagination to entertain the younger ones with stories about a taniwha, Tinakrifa, a ghostly spirit who haunted our house. The house lent itself to ghost stories – not because it was tumbledown and full of cobwebs, but because it had a dark cupboard under the stairs that resonated with a moaning noise when wind blew across the top of the tall furnace flue. It also had a lot of built-in furniture full of nooks and crannies where scary creatures might hide.

At that time, we were living in New Zealand, where the government had launched a program to improve cross-cultural awareness of the indigenous Maori people. Maori language, legends, and beliefs formed part of a cultural studies curriculum at Tegan's school. What a great way to fire up a child's naturally fertile imagination! Tegan responded by creating the taniwha, Tinakrifa, as the resident ghostly spirit of our house.

In Maori mythology, taniwha were supernatural creatures, similar to serpents and dragons. They liked to hide in rivers, waterholes, lakes or caves. They could slither around like lizards or snakes, and some could fly with wings or swim with fins. Some were responsible for creating land forms, a bit like the Rainbow Serpent of Aboriginal mythology. The two taniwha, Ngake and Whataitai, for example, created the channel that now links Wellington harbour to the sea.

Taniwha could be friendly and protective of local people, or malevolent and vengeful, especially to people who broke rules of tapu. They were also a useful cautionary presence for children near water.

Tegan's Tinakrifa was a shape-shifter who could change his size and appear as either a dragon-like bird or a fish. He had good and bad moods depending on the weather. Warm sunshine encouraged him out into the garden to swim lazily in the fish pond along with the goldfish. On the hottest days, he might be lurking like a lizard under bushes in the shade. Cold weather, and particularly wind, saw him retreating into the cupboard under the stairs and moaning in misery. This was not a good time to annoy him!

When Tegan was ready to tell stories to her little siblings, she herded them into the dark cupboard under the stairs, closed the door and used a small penlight torch shining up from under her chin to create a dark, ghostly ambience. Little sister Tina, aged six, was a natural sceptic. She sometimes helped to embroider the tall tales for extra authenticity. Their two little brothers, aged four and five, were susceptible enough to believe in taniwha spirits at the time. Leo the youngest, however, soon abandoned all that stuff along with Santa Claus and the tooth fairy.

Five-year-old Nathan was particularly open to ghostly and spiritual tales. I remember him bursting out of the storytelling cupboard with big round eyes looking for the taniwha, and a voice following from the cupboard saying, 'Look out! Tinakrifa will get you. He's not happy. You can hear him moaning.'

For Nathan, these tales of Tinakrifa had a lasting impact. During a quick visit from his work in Sydney, we were reminiscing about the features of our old home in New Zealand. When I asked him if, now aged forty-six, he still remembered the cupboard under the stairs, he put his head down in his hands and said, 'Bloody Tinakrifa! That house was haunted for sure!'

It's interesting to look back on kids' games in terms of the clues they might have held to their future lives. These days, Tegan, the teller of stories, has set up her own creative web blog. Tina is a trained counsellor and psychologist who helps people with improving their personal realities. After his early school years, the only flights of fancy taken by Leo, the youngest, were probably induced by nefarious chemical substances! He is unlikely to be exposing his own young son to Santa, the Tooth Fairy, or taniwha spirits any time soon.

Nathan, however, has become a bit of a shape-shifter himself. He's a TV and movie actor, using his significant powers of imagination and mimicry to good advantage. Still strongly influenced by Maori culture, he observes a number of Maori spiritual rituals, somewhat similar in intent to the smoking ceremonies of Aboriginal culture. I suspect that one day his own kids may be playing taniwha games.

The highs and lows of high tea

'Mum,' said David, looking up from his book, 'what's high tea?

The kids in this story are having high tea in the nursery with their nurse and governess. It says Robert the eldest is nearly old enough to go to dinner, but he can't go until he can wear long pants. What is that all about?'

'Well, dear,' replied Mother from the kitchen bench, 'that's a very old book, and I think it's talking about an even older and very snobby time in England when people were either upper class or working class. The upper class owned all the property and had a lot of money, and the working class were poor and mainly worked for the upper class as servants and labourers in hard physical jobs. Many upper-class families had two houses, one in the country with a lot of farmland, and one in the city. Their houses usually had a lot of servants.

'Upper-class women didn't do much except order the servants around and do ladylike things like music and flower paintings. During the winter half of the year, when families were in their town houses, ladies spent a lot of time visiting each other to gossip about the latest scandals and plan the best possible marriages for their children. The marriage market needed a lot of formal dinners, balls and other supervised social events to show the young ladies and gentlemen off to each other.

'Upper-class men spent their time in the country supervising their farm labourers, who usually lived on or near their land in little villages. In the times we're talking about, farm crops and animals made a lot of money for the land owners. When they were living in the city, the men spent lots of time in gentlemen's clubs, talking about money, and often doing a lot of drinking and gambling.'

'How do you know all that?' chimed in Caroline, David's older sister, from the sofa where she was doing an assignment online. 'You're not old enough to have been there.'

'I've read a lot of books about those times,' said Mother.

Caro sniffed and said, 'A lot of lurid Regency novels, I bet!'

'But what was "high tea"?' David reminded Mother.

'It was the sort of tea we have every night at the kitchen table when Dad gets home from work,' responded Mother. 'You know – meat, veg and then dessert. But it would have been a lot more boring in those days, with lots of stodgy stuff like mashed potatoes, pea soup, boiled cabbage, and tapioca pudding or bread and jam. In those days, they'd never heard of stir-fry, pizza, burgers or pasta.'

'But why did they call it high tea?' persisted David. 'We just call it tea or dinner.'

Mother thought for a moment. 'I think it was to distinguish it from afternoon tea, which was something the ladies had around four in the afternoon to tide them over till dinner. They were usually sitting around in easy chairs gossiping. Servants came in and served little fancy cakes and sandwiches on low tables, like our coffee table, and cups of tea were poured from fancy teapots into little fine china cups.'

Now it was David's turn to think for a moment. 'But didn't they ruin their appetite for dinner? You always tell us not to eat anything after half-past three in case we ruin our appetite.'

'Well, in those days,' said Mother, dinner wasn't served till at least eight o'clock and usually went on till about ten o'clock or later. It was a grown-up occasion and everyone had to put on formal dinner suits and evening dresses before coming to the table. That's why children had to have high tea, using a high table and chairs in the nursery. Besides, it was really just another lesson. The governess was responsible for teaching them proper table manners, and the nurse was keeping an eye on them to ensure they learned how to eat the right amounts of the right things.'

'What a bore,' chimed in Caro. 'I'm so glad I didn't live in those days.'

'There were a few good points,' said Mother. 'The cook used to send up nice leftover cakes from afternoon tea for dessert at high tea.'

David still had a question. 'Did servants and poor people have late dinners too?'

'No,' said Mother. 'They had to get up too early, and work too hard and too long for that. They had only high tea, served in the kitchen when the man of the house came home from work, just like we do today.'

David wondered whether that meant his family were working class, but he thought the better of asking that question.

I like flowers

I like flowers. I also enjoy, admire and respect them; and the jokers amongst them set me laughing in sheer humorous enjoyment. As Elizabeth Barrett Browning said in a famous sonnet, 'How do I love thee? Let me count the ways.' So let me try to expand the simple statement 'I like flowers'.

I love colourful flowers, flowers with rampant, standout visibility in a sea of green or brown. It can be one delicate point of perfect colour. Think of one perfect magenta orchid in a rainforest, one gracefully curved white lily in a vase, or one golden dandelion in a smooth, green lawn. It can be a fabulous feast of colour swathed across a whole tree or whole landscape. Think of the tossing violet crown of a big tropical Jacaranda tree, the delicate pink rain of petals from a walkway of Japanese cherry trees, or the solid, rippling, golden carpet of a broad-acre canola crop. The endless variety of flower colours is stunning.

I love the perfumes of flowers; the delight of bringing a flower, or a bunch of flowers, up to my nose and breathing in the classic scent of traditional roses, the springtime perfume of jonquils, or the fascinating earthy, mushroom-like scent of gardenias; and I love the sweet, heavy perfume of evening flowers, like the drowsy scent of jasmine enjoyed with a shared bottle of wine on the veranda at dusk.

I respect the true purpose of flowers. Their colours and perfumes are not just for my enjoyment, but intimately woven into plant lives. They provide pollinating insects, birds, or bats with sweet, energy-giving nectar and protein in exchange for carrying fertilising pollen. Their colours, shapes and perfumes attract the right pollinator, and patterns on the petals, help guide the pollinator into the business region of the flower where it can pick up both pollen and a reward. These bee guides are a bit like airport lights that guide planes in to land. How clever is that!

I am in awe of the scams and trickery incorporated into some plant-pollinator interactions. Think of a water lily, such an innocent-looking, beautiful, ancient flower. It opens to the sun on the first day, attracting many insects to come and drink the copious nectar. When they are too sated to fly away, the flower closes and imprisons them for the night, covering them with pollen in the process. The next day, the flower opens again, liberating them to fly off, covered with pollen, to find the next day's food in another flower.

And consider a leggy, ragged-looking spider orchid with long, skinny, dark petals hanging off the edges of the flower like insect legs. It looks at first glance like a leggy wasp sitting on the top of a stem. No sweet floral perfume here! Any nearby male pollinator wasp smells the enticing, sexy scent of a female wasp. Awkwardly, he tries to mate with the flower, getting walloped over the head with sticky pollen for his pains. But does he learn a lesson? No. He flies off, carrying the pollen, to try the same mating trick with the next spider orchid. It's a sad tale of unrequited love with no reward. Only the flowers benefit.

I laugh at the jokers in the pack. Humans assume flowers have sweet, pleasant or interesting perfumes; but how about rotting meat for a change! From the plant's point of view, there's nothing wrong with co-opting blowflies and corpse beetles to do the work in place of in-nocuous honey bees. After all, if you're a plant that flowers at ground level in a forest, why bother to try attracting bees that are working in the tops of the trees. Nature is not stupid! What makes the most dis-tinctive, arresting aroma at ground level? Dead animals, of course; and there are some plants that take advantage.

Rafflesia is a parasitic, tropical plant that lives on the roots of a jungle vine. Its flower develops underground and then opens like a giant, flat, stinkpot on the forest floor, up to eighty or a hundred centimetres across. It even looks a bit like rotting meat with its purplish-red colour and whitish flecks like blobs of fat. Blowflies, attracted from miles around carry the stinking, sticky, pollen-containing secretion off to the next flower.

Another huge stinkpot is the titan arum, *Amorphophallus*. Shaped like a gargantuan, stocky arum lily, it rises nearly two metres up from the forest floor. It has a central sticky, yellowish or purplish, pollen-bearing, spike surrounded by a frilled purple spathe. The corpse-like stench is execrable! Blowflies arrive in their thousands!

When it comes to these two massive, malodorous flowers, the joke is well and truly on us. They may stink, but I still love them for their trickery and sheer cleverness.

The tragedy of a button

As we were clearing out the old family home, we came across a battered old brown cabin trunk of the type formerly used on ocean liners. It carried a stained and faded label written in our father's handwriting: 'Hugh Douglas Gordon, passenger to Hobart, Tasmania.' It wasn't locked, so we lifted the hasp and cautiously opened it. Inside was a mix of old books, papers and photo albums full of small black-and-white photos of many places and people our dad had met and seen on his way to Tasmania from Scotland in 1937.

There was also a big brown envelope addressed to Hugh D. Gordon c/o Miss Gall at an unfamiliar Edinburgh location. We decided it must be where he boarded as a student while he attended the University of Edinburgh. The contents were several faded carbon copies of a typed short story by Gordon Hughes, a couple of letters of submission to local ladies' journals dated 1931, and a couple of very polite letters of rejection from the journal editors. It seemed our father, as an impoverished nineteen-year-old first-year student, had been trying to earn some pocket money.

I carefully unfolded one of the carbon copies, shaking rust flakes off the eighty-eight-year-old paper clip, and read the story out loud

*

I knew I was in for it the moment I saw him, striding across the office with a newspaper in his hand and looking as though he must have it out with someone or burst.

I had just risen to go home, but I sat down again. I always sat down when Wiffle elected to talk to me.

'What do you think of this?' he snorted, hurling the offending periodical on my desk. 'A woman grousing about the unequal privileges of the sexes! A woman, mark you! Why, man, they can't leave us anything at all. They go in for all our sports, they go into business, no matter what we do they ape us. But if we try any of their stunts – cooking, sewing, even sweeping a floor – why, they laugh at us. They do indeed! They say that only women can do these things. What utter bosh!'

'Yes,' I replied weakly, with a nervous glance at the clock, but I had said one word too many. Thus encouraged, he plunged in again.

'I tell you what, we married men could give them an eye-opener. We ought to fend for ourselves, do our own sewing and whatnot. They'd soon see they're not indispensable. Why, if you or I…'

'Look here,' I butted in, 'if we must have it, let's have it on the way home. We've just time to catch our bus.'

So we fled. The bus was actually moving as we skidded round the bend. Wiffle fell on any-old-how. I boarded it in a single bound, worthy of a champion hurdler, but disaster overtook me in the moment of triumph. I felt a telltale jerk in the small of my back, and wheeling round placed my foot on the button as it rattled to the floor.

'By Jove!' whooped Wiffle as we sat down. 'This is a heaven-sent chance to put our idea into practice.'

I let the plural possessive pass unchallenged.

'Not a word of this to your wife. Sew it on yourself and tell her afterwards. Let me know tomorrow how she takes it.'

I was none too enthusiastic, so he hastened to reassure me.

'It's child's play, man. I know if I'd been in your place…'

'All right,' said I, 'just you come round to my place after tea and lend a hand. I can let you in without the wife knowing.'

After tea – more hurried than usual – I retired to my room, changed my trousers, and sought out Dorothy's work box. The idea of calling such a simple job work! Then I slipped downstairs to admit Wiffle. Like a pair of conspirators we tiptoed to the scene of operations.

Of course I got the work to do. Wiffle knew all about it, so he had to act as director. I piloted the needle safely through the button and pulled the thread in its wake – right out. Well, how was I to know when to stop pulling?

Then I had a brilliant idea. I tied a knot in the end of the thread so that it could not slip through. It gave me some satisfaction to reflect that a woman's intellect could not have devised such a scheme. And for that matter neither had Wiffle.

At my next attempt, I drew out the needle confidently, but to my chagrin, the other end of the thread slipped out of the needle eye. After some delay, it was restored and I returned the needle without mishap through one of the other holes. Elated by this success, I tried again.

This time, I rammed the button amidships. Then suddenly the needle leapt out and viciously stabbed my left hand. Well, I ask you!

'Bad luck, old man!' said Wiffle. 'Try again.'

I grunted expressively and went downstairs. 'Dorothy,' I began, parading for inspection my most tactful and ingratiating smile, 'I can't understand how any man would be a bachelor from choice. I'm sure I could never get along without you.'

She returned my smile, but – cynically? No, surely not. I must have been mistaken there. Perhaps it was a trick of the firelight.

'Well?' she prompted.

'Oh, by the way,' I remarked, apropos of nothing, 'I had an unfortunate accident today. I boarded the bus rather hurriedly and a button fell off my trousers.'

A smile of enlightenment spread over her face. 'Bring them along. It won't take me a minute.'

When I returned, I found her, to my amazement, tying a knot in the end of a thread. I handed her the trousers with a nonchalant air. Imagine my horror when, with a delighted chuckle, she held up a black thread, knotted at one end and at least two yards long – my thread.

'Oh, you men! You vain, clever men! I wondered what was on when I saw you slipping upstairs with Charlie Wiffle. Watch closely and I'll show you how to do it!'

I didn't. I went to look for Wiffle, but he'd gone.

We could hear our father in the story, albeit at a rather unsophisticated stage. Two of his main characteristics were a dry, Scottish sense of humour, and a rather modern appreciation of gender equality and the place of women in society. We could sense both of these developing in this early attempt at creative writing.

Gone, but not forgotten

There it stands: a big block of a building, full frontal on the main approach to the University of Kentucky, with large lettering across its face, just below the roof, proclaiming, 'The Maxwell H. Gluck Equine Research Centre'. Unforgettable! Engineered to be remembered for the name of its principal donor, a wealthy horse farmer! Well, this is Kentucky after all, home of the Kentucky Derby, and home of the famous yearling sales where wealthy Saudi Arabians and even the Queen of England have been seen amongst the bidding audiences.

But why mark a building so massively with one's name? Surely a more conventional brass nameplate in the lobby would have been sufficient to acknowledge a generous bequest? It seems the name 'Gluck' must stand 'out-and-proud', to be remembered as long as the building stands. Do people like Maxwell H. Gluck fear being forgotten after they are gone?

Most of us would like to imagine being personally remembered by immediate family – children, grandchildren, perhaps great-grandchildren – and our own close friends. But surely most of us are less interested in being remembered by wider social groups. What drives those who seek to become legends? Do they fear that being forgotten means their lives were irrelevant? What about those who write their own tombstone epitaphs or obituaries to control the narrative of societal memories?

Some individuals become memorable – even the stuff of legend – by their deeds, works, or achievements in life. Think of Joan of Arc, Leonardo da Vinci, or Sir Edmund Hillary. Many such 'heroes' may not even be seeking to be remembered – only to achieve an objective.

But what of those who do aim to be broadly remembered forever? Many historical rulers erected statues of themselves to underscore their claimed importance and make sure their memory lived on beyond their lifetimes. Ramses the Great of Egypt, for example, not only sought eternal life in the hereafter, but also to be remembered by the living forever. Since we still see his statues more than three thousand years after he died, he did pretty well. Creating aides-memoire in stone, as he did, was undoubtedly far more effective than our use of fragile paper books, film and digital media today. How about the beautiful limestone bust of Queen Nefertiti or the fabulous golden death mask of Tutankhamun – definitely unforgettable!

So much for striving to be remembered. But is it all worth it? You can actually become memorable for thousands to millions of years without even trying. All you need to do is die in circumstances which deep-freeze or mummify your corpse, or fossilise your bones.

Tollund Man is a 'bog body' from Danish Jutland. He died by strangulation around two and a half thousand years ago, but his beautifully preserved face looks as serene and peaceful as if in sleep. Even the stubble on the skin of his jaw is visible. He, and other 'bog bodies' from across northern Europe, were mummified by the cold acid waters of sphagnum peat bogs where they were deliberately buried after ritual sacrifice. They give us a 'memory' of how they looked, what they ate and how they met their death through pagan ritual.

Ötzi the Ice Man, found emerging from melting ice in a Tyrolean alpine stream, now lies in a museum and provides memories of not only his appearance but also his clothes, tools and a fatal arrow injury suffered some five thousand years ago, just as a glacial period engulfed the mountains where he fell.

Turkana Boy, however, is the memory champion. Suffering septicaemia from a tooth abscess, and also from a herniated disc in his back, he died at the age of about thirteen around one and a half million years ago, his body falling into the water of a shallow lake where it was buried under mud and his bones fossilised. His remarkably well preserved skeleton comes from the absolute dawn of humanity – from the time of transition from Homo erectus to Homo sapiens.

Which leads to a final point: whether we like it or not, our genetic inheritance is a biological 'memory' over long periods of time. Who we are today was written into our genes by our forebears, and will be passed on to our descendants as long as humanity survives on Earth. In the great evolutionary story, we will be gone, but our genes will make sure we are not forgotten.

If I were Santa Claus

The lead-up to Christmas is well-named 'Silly Season'. If I were Santa Claus, I would put an end to our society's outrageously consumerist Christmas culture. I would stop all the commercial encouragement of greed and self-indulgence. I would get rid of nasty, junky plastic toys that break within a week or so, and I'd do away with all the over-the-top wrappings and trappings that just finish up in the rubbish.

I would stop all the driving around on Christmas Day to have coffee, lunch and dinner at different family homes. It's just an invitation to waste fossil fuel and generate more stress and traffic bingles! And I would put airfares way up for the Christmas period to discourage all the wasteful interstate visits as well.

Christmas has become TOO much – spend spend spend, rush rush rush, gobble gobble gobble, glug, glug, glug! Many family members and friends who push themselves to get together don't actually want to. You'd be surprised how many of them don't even enjoy the occasion. Christmas is infamous for family quarrels and bouts of depression. Why not just do away with it and spread family interactions out over the year? Christmas, for the great majority of folks, no longer has anything to do with celebrating the birthday of a man who famously promoted love, simplicity, and poverty.

Imagine me with young children sitting on my knee in Santa's grotto in the lead-up to Christmas.

'Hello, young Jimmy. What do you want for Christmas?'

'I want an electric scooter, an X-Box, and an iPad please, Santa.'

'You greedy young pup!' Think of how long someone would have to work to buy all that. How about a junior toolkit instead? Then you could learn how to make things and be useful round the house.'

Or 'Hello, young Jennifer. What would you like for Christmas?'

'I want a folding flip phone in its own pink handbag please, Santa. And some shoes with lights that flash when I walk, new pink jeans, and a bigger make-up kit than Mary has.'

'You vain little minx! What makes you think all that will improve the way you look? And how will Mary feel if you go round flaunting your present as bigger than hers? How about a sketchbook and water-colours for doing something more positive than painting your face?'

Well, of course I'm not really Santa, and never likely to get a chance to even pretend. You've probably met me long ago in the Dr Seuss storybook and movie called *How the Grinch stole Christmas*. They were all about my other attempts to fix the Christmas problem. You probably think I'm a horrible old gnome who hates people enjoying themselves but, actually, you'd be wrong.

I would so very much like to see folks enjoying Christmas Day in the spirit of 'elegant sufficiency', laughing and happy because their expectations are not over the top, and can be readily met or exceeded. What about giving just one or two presents of the sort that are really needed, durable and creative – presents lovingly wrapped in salvaged paper or a recycled container? What about just one or two really appreciated treats with Christmas dinner, not an overladen pig-fest of luxury stuff to generate more obesity. And what about busting stress levels by staying in one place for the day and visiting the other rellies or friends next year?

Yes, I want folks to enjoy Christmas, but I also want kids of all ages to spare a thought for who really pays for it all in the end – not Mum and Dad, not Grandma and Grandpa, not friends, not Santa – but our beautiful green and blue Earth. There's a very good reason why my movie shows me with green skin. I was getting ready to come out as who I really am – the Green Grinch!

Know me from what I wear

'Hello, Lindy. It's nice to meet you at last. I have heard so much about you from your grandma over the years, I feel as though I have known you forever. Do you know who I am?'

I dropped my school bag and plopped down into a chair opposite the elderly woman sitting on the sofa. 'You must be my Great-auntie Mavis, Grandma's sister. Mum said you were coming to stay for a few weeks till your new unit is ready.'

'That's right, dear. How about you go and get comfortable with a snack and we can get to know each other better.'

I brushed the stray hair off my face, picked up my bag and made for the door. Then I remembered my manners. 'Auntie, would you like a cup of tea?'

'Yes thanks, Lindy. That would be nice. I like it with milk and one sugar.'

I ran to my room, tossed my bag on the bed, changed into jeans and a T-shirt, and then went to the kitchen to make tea. I was soon back in the lounge with a tea tray and a plate of biscuits. I set the tray down in front of Auntie Mavis.

'Thank you, Lindy. That looks lovely. I'll pour the tea while you have a biscuit and look me over as a start to getting to know me. What can you tell about me from what you can see?'

Well, this was unusual. I was used to grown-ups telling me stuff about themselves, not asking me to guess. But it seemed like a fun game.

I looked Auntie over while she poured tea. 'Well,' I began, 'I can see from your loose, floaty dress that you like to feel relaxed in your clothes. I think that means you're a relaxed kind of person. The bold flower pattern and frilly neckline say you like flowers, but also that you like to be noticed rather than hiding in the background; and I'm guessing your favourite colours are violet and pink. Am I right so far?'

'Yes, right on the money, Lindy. When I was a high-school teacher my nickname was Petunia. I wasn't supposed to know, but of course I heard it sometimes. What else can you see?

'Well, your dress is quite long, so I think you must hate wearing stockings as much as I do. Your shoes have low heels, so I think that means you prefer to be comfortable. They look clean and well-polished so I think, while you like to look relaxed, you don't want to be scruffy. The gold locket round your neck could have something precious in it you like to keep close to you. You aren't wearing a wedding ring, but I already know from Grandma you're a Miss not a Mrs. Your other rings, bracelets and earrings tell me you like shiny, sparkly things. How am I doing?'

'Really well, dear. You've realised that what I wear says lots about me as a person. Yes, I've never married, more's the pity, but I once had a fiancé. He was killed in the Vietnam War, and I've always regretted that terrible waste of his life. The precious thing in my locket is his photo. Now, if you look at other things about me, what can you tell?'

I think you like to look natural because you're not wearing make-up and your hair isn't tinted to hide the grey. It's also longish, a bit wild like mine, and escaping from its clip, so you're not a neat-freak.

Auntie laughed. 'Oh, Lindy, you are doing so well. I would hate to try to hide anything from you.'

I laughed too. This was fun. 'I'm not finished yet, Auntie. Your handbag down there beside you is really big for a lady's bag, so I think you must like to carry stuff with you in case.'

Auntie bent over, opened the bag, and took out two books. 'Good guess, Lindy. These are what I use to keep track of phone numbers, appointments and thoughts about the things I see, do and read. I know I could get rid of them if I got a fancy mobile phone with all those "app" things, but I like the old way of doing it, even though it's a bit heavier to carry around. Any last thoughts?'

'Well, Auntie, you're very easy to talk to, so I think you must really like people. I've enjoyed our game, and I feel like I know you quite well already.'

*

I have often thought of this conversation over the years. It taught me a lot about how to use observation and deduction. It probably led to getting my job as a police detective. I think Auntie Mavis must have been a great high-school teacher!

The night the lights went out

From around 2000 to 2003, we lived on the hill above the Marino Rocks café in southern Adelaide. We loved the wonderful view across Gulf St Vincent, the sea in all its moods, and the spectacular sunsets. From our deck, we could see up the coast to Seacliff, Brighton and beyond. At that time, the seascape was active with small coastal tankers coming and going at the former Port Stanvac oil refinery. We could read their names with binoculars, see the activity on their decks and, if we were lucky, also see occasional pods of dolphins patrolling the rocky coast below. Once, as though we had been catapulted back in time, we saw the *Endeavour* replica sailing majestically past towards Port Adelaide. There were no such romantic feelings, however, for the sight of an ominous, black Collins-class submarine quietly motoring past

On one of those very hot Adelaide summer days, the temperature had been over forty for most of the day and was still over thirty at ten o'clock in the evening. It was breathless – not even a whisper of breeze. We were sitting in the lounge, close to our only air conditioner trying to endure the discomfort, and wondering whether we would need to bring our bedding into the lounge for the night in order to sleep.

Suddenly the lights went out. The TV died, the fridge stopped working and the air conditioner went off. Silence! Oh no! It was one of Adelaide's infamous rolling summer blackouts. The electricity grid had been overwhelmed by the impact of air conditioning throughout the city. We knew we would probably have two hours to wait before the rolling blackout rolled on to another suburb, so we went out onto the deck hoping that a milder breeze might develop in the meantime.

It was strange to see the whole length of our coastal view made visible only by moonlight on the wavelets of the calm sea. There were no street lights and no window lights anywhere north or south of us. It felt like the primeval silence and darkness of an ancient land.

But wait – there was one small lighted window north of us on the hill face at Seacliff. How could that be?

By coincidence, I had the answer. Some months previously, I had attended a seminar on Future Energy Systems at the University of Adelaide Waite Campus. Dr Barbara Hardy, attending as a campus patron, spoke briefly about her own domestic energy project. She described twelve-volt lighting powered by car batteries and solar panels. The lone light at Seacliff must be her house. A quick check of phone and street directories confirmed that it had to be the case.

Remember that famous line from the café scene in the movie *When Harry met Sally*: 'I'll have what she's having'? That night of the blackout, John and I decided on the spot that we would have what she (Barbara Hardy) was having. To hell with the all-too-frequent power cuts and summer blackouts!

At the time, we were involved in designing a home in the Arts Eco-Village at Aldinga further south on the gulf coast, so we had a chance to incorporate our new objective. It was not straightforward. Back then, very few entrepreneurs were selling solar systems, and even fewer were dealing with battery-backed options. Emergency twelve-volt lighting connected to car batteries was one thing, but we wanted backup for everything other than the oven and cooktop. We were tired, not only of the lights going out, but also of power cuts affecting our fridge, TV, kettle and computers. This was a different ball game. It meant using solar panels with inverters and substantial batteries to back the 240-volt system of our whole house for hours at a time.

Finally, we found a contractor who was able to install a suitable system. Although it was less efficient and more expensive than today's equivalent systems, it really paid off. We had NO ELECTRICITY BILLS – and NO POWER CUTS – from the time we moved into the house. The system has also paid for itself several times over in the intervening years.

And there was a humorous vote of approval from a teenage member of a school group visiting our home in the early days. When he realised we never had power cuts and could run our computers without interruption, he said, 'I want come and live at your place!'

As a bonus, we have now also dispensed with petrol bills thanks to a small fully electric vehicle that charges directly from solar panels.

And a final point to ponder: if self-funded retirees like us invest in the stock market, we have to pay tax on dividends. But the tax man is only interested in what we earn, not what we save, so the savings on our electricity bills were untaxed. Consequently, our advice to the other self-funded retirees around us was to 'put your investment on the roof!'

Resilience: moving on

Janet frowned into her glass of wine. There was nothing wrong with the drink. It was her usual Friday-night pub treat. There was nothing wrong with the conversation either. This was the usual Friday Club of four old friends sharing a drink after work. But there was definitely something 'off' about the day – well, what else could one say about being fired at five o'clock on a Friday!

If she was truthful, it didn't come completely out of the blue. It had been building in the background for some time.

The job that she had studied so long and worked so hard for just didn't cut it. If she was truthful, her job sucked, and for the last several months she had, without even admitting it to herself, been exhausted by long working hours and bored stiff by their content. When she started her legal assistant job in a large law firm, it was supposedly the path to becoming a barrister and ultimately a legal partner in the firm. Her parents, who saw law as a prestigious career, were delighted when she got her position.

What she hadn't expected was the firm's fixation on billable hours to the exclusion of any human aspects of the job. Every minute of client consultation, in the office or on the phone, had to be written up for billing. The other strong emphasis was on processing as many clients as possible, whether they fitted into a reasonable working day or not. There was no time to explore the human aspects of clients' circumstances. It was just a relentless search to find appropriate clauses of law and draft legal briefs to hand on to appropriate senior lawyers.

Janet knew the work was a necessary apprenticeship, but over time she had realised that she lacked the necessary interest in law to make it all worthwhile. Lately, her billing hours had slipped, and she had started to make excuses for not seeking extra hours. The acrimonious end of a workplace relationship with another junior lawyer had also taken its toll. All in all, being fired was just part of an all-round bad workplace experience. She frowned into her drink while her friends' conversation washed over her.

'Hey, Janet,' said Clare after some minutes, 'are you OK? You're very quiet tonight. How's the law business?'

'It stinks,' said Janet succinctly. 'I just got fired, all of half an hour ago.'

Well, that killed the cheerful conversation! Janet now had the undivided attention of the whole group.

'Oh, poor you!' 'You must be so upset.' 'How awful after years of study and working so hard.' 'What went wrong?'

'It feels like a slap in the face,' said Janet, 'but, to be honest, I think if I were the practice manager, I would have fired me too. I just couldn't get motivated to log enough billable hours. My pride's hurt of course, and I have no idea how I'm going to confess to Mum and Dad, let alone go home to live with them if I can't find another way to pay rent. After losing both job and boyfriend, this feels like rock bottom.'

Jenny clinked her glass for attention and said, 'But you know the only way the road can go from rock bottom is…' She paused and, taking their cue, the others shouted, 'UP!' and raised their glasses in a toast.

Janet looked around the table with a few tears threatening to fall. 'Thanks, guys. You're the best friends anyone could have. I'm going to need your moral support in the next few months while I find the road to UP. First I need to find some sort of job to pay rent and bills while I organise what I want to do long-term. And believe me, another job in a law practice is not going to be on the list in spite of anything my parents say! The first step is to 'fess up to Mum and Dad, and then deal with the job and flat situation.'

'Wait a minute,' said Val, leaning across the table. 'There might be a better way. When Robbie and I went to that great new restaurant, Oyster Bay, in Trenton Street on Wednesday night, they had a card in the window advertising for staff. I think there was a position like hostess or receptionist going. You could do that, Janet. You're a good people person. Why don't you walk round there and talk to them now.'

So that's how Janet walked out of a misfit job on a Friday, faced up to reality and walked into another utterly different job the following Monday. She has never looked back. Now, as restaurant and cellar-door manager for a major winery, she loves the fact that her workplace is filled with relaxed happy people catering to relaxed happy guests.

The limit of friendship

Dot and I met on our first day of high school, when we both finished up in the same class. We discovered we could travel to and from school together on public transport, and later began to spend other time together in typical teenage activities.

It was an unexpected friendship. I was a 'goody-two-shoes' who mostly behaved as instructed. Dot was different. She was bored by school, skipped homework, or did a token amount in the breaks between classes. The teachers were frustrated by her attitude, but encouragement to 'try harder' made no impression. She had no respect for work she regarded as stupid or boring.

Eventually, however, the problem was sorted out by our Latin teacher.

On this occasion, after being given Latin translation for homework, the whole class had done poorly. We were berated for laziness, and given a snap translation test. Dot finished first, handed her paper to the teacher and walked out of the room. Grimly, the test proceeded until we had all finished.

Next day, an incredulous teacher told us Dot had topped the class. On being asked why she couldn't perform like this regularly, Dot just shrugged. The teachers got the message. Dot was bright but unchallenged and bored by normal lessons. In those days, there were no special provisions for gifted students, so life continued as before but teachers no longer worried about Dot. They knew if she was in the classroom she was learning and left her to get on with it.

At the end of our fourth year, we were both accredited for university entrance. Dot elected to leave school and begin an arts degree, while I decided to stay another year to take more science and maths.

Our paths now diverged but we still met regularly in a local coffee bar. As bored by university lectures as she had been by school, Dot soon dropped out and enrolled at a secretarial college. It seemed like a backward step, but because graduation depended on achievement rather than time invested, it soon paid off. With a letter recommending her as the year's top graduate, it didn't take her long to find a job.

Over the next few years, the spaces in our friendship grew longer, first as we both married and had children, then when I moved to jobs in another city and subsequently overseas. We always found, however, that when we did manage to get together, the intervening time disappeared and we were able to catch up with each other's news, much as we had done through school. We still felt like friends in spite of our different lives.

Dot carried on being Dot. Bored with her first office job, she moved to working for an actuary and valuer. Around the same time, she took the entry test for Mensa, the high-IQ organisation. Much to Mensa's surprise, she aced this test too with one of the highest national scores. She was amused to be the only secretary ever admitted to Mensa, probably embarrassing the organisation in the process!

That wasn't all. As an additional challenge, she used her boss's text books to learn the actuary and valuing business, ultimately qualifying to become junior partner in the business. This still wasn't enough for Dot. She began buying old houses, renovating while living in them, and selling them for profit, using her valuer experience to design financially rewarding improvements.

We were not good correspondents, but for years we had quite a good intermittent friendship by simply picking up where we had left off after the last visit. Sadly, though, it couldn't last. During a visit when we were in our forties, Dot confided that she had been diagnosed with terminal ovarian cancer. What a shock. We wept together and did some reminiscing about life. I felt totally inadequate to help her with such devastating news. What a terrible tragedy that such a bright mind was to be snuffed out so soon.

Eventually, I had to return to a dependent family and job half a world away, leaving Dot to face the end. I badly regretted that final goodbye, knowing her need for support would grow. Fortunately, she had a guardian angel next door. Dennis was in his sixties, and had recently lost his partner. My first impression of him was a 'funny old stick', but as Dot became incapacitated, he took on the role of informal carer. Right up to the point where she entered a hospice two weeks before her death, he provided meals, home help, personal care and moral support. Dennis was a gem!

The Dutch have a saying: 'A good neighbour is better than a faraway friend.' Sadly, in light of how I had to leave Dot in her time of need, I have to agree.